The One I Stood Beside

PIPER RAYNE

About The One I Stood Beside

It's the classic story— best friends since childhood agree to a fake marriage, thinking they can pretend to love each other without their relationship changing.

Jude would do anything for me. He's stood by my side since we were six, and I've done the same for him.

When my father dies, leaving our family farm drowning in debt and on the brink of being auctioned, I'm not surprised Jude steps in to help. I just never dreamed he'd fall to bended knee and devise a plan for us to fool everyone into thinking there's more than a lifelong friendship between us.

Soon, I'm moving into his house, we're planning a wedding on his family's ranch, and we discover a new side to our relationship. I keep reminding myself it's not real—it's only to secure a loan to save the farm.

I've secretly loved Jude all my life, and now that I know how good we are together, I'm not sure we can return to being just friends.

THE ONE I
Stood Beside

The Noughton Family
Parents
Bruce and Daisy (deceased) Noughton
Children
Ben Noughton – Gillian Adams
(*The One I Left Behind*)
Jude Noughton – Sadie Wilkins
(*The One I Stood Beside*)
Emmett Noughton – Briar Adams
(*The One I Didn't See Coming*)

The Owens Family
Parents
Brad and Darla Owens
Children
Lottie Owens
Bennett Owens
Romy Owens

The Ellis Family
Parents
Wade and Bette Ellis
Children
Poppy Ellis
Jensen Ellis
Scarlett Ellis

To see more of the Plain Daisy Ranch family tree
visit our website:
https://piperrayne.com/noughton-family-tree

Prologue

SIX YEARS OLD

Cock-a-doodle-do

Rooster Phil is up. I roll over in bed, looking out the window. The sky is yellow and orange, so I guess it's okay to get up.

"Benny," I whisper to my little brother in the bunk above me.

He doesn't answer.

I'm always the first one awake now. I miss Mommy so much more in the morning. She was always the first one up. I never heard her go downstairs, but the smell of coffee or bacon would wake me. Or my dad's cowboy boots when he went downstairs.

Benny wouldn't wake up until Mom had been in our room at least three times, and Emmett was still in his crib, stuck until Mom went to get him.

The back screen door would bang when Dad left to work the ranch, and he wouldn't come home until the sun was falling.

But now, there's no coffee brewing.

There's no bacon sizzling in the pan.

My dad's boots haven't walked down our stairs since we buried Mommy.

I crawl out of bed and pull on the dirty jeans from my hamper and toss on a T-shirt and my Noughton Ranch sweatshirt in case it's cold. I stop at the door, and I look to make sure Benny is still sleeping. He's on his stomach, his arms tucked under his pillow. One leg out from the blanket.

I tiptoe down the hall even though I don't think I need to worry about waking anyone. My dad never comes out of his room anymore. When Emmett wakes up, I'm the one who gets him now.

I skip over the squeaking stair, but my socks slide on the hardwood, and I fall down two steps before grabbing the railing to stop myself. I wait and listen. As always, no movement. Our house used to be crazy. Now it's like I live at the library Mommy used to take us boys to in town.

Picking up my boots, I carry them through the back door, slowly shutting the screen door so it doesn't bang. On the back porch, I put on my cowboy boots and sneak off.

I'll be back before Aunt Darla comes to make us breakfast.

A few trucks pull down the drive, workers starting their day.

Instead of following the path around the farm, I hike through the trees along the edge of the small lake in the middle of our property. The horses are out grazing, which means someone is already here, so I don't pet them. I don't want anyone knowing where I'm going.

I climb the hill to the fenced-off area where generations of my family are buried.

I sit on the ground at the far end of the fresh mound of dirt and stare at the simple cross. Aunt Bette said she'll have a tombstone like Grandpa's in a few weeks.

I stare at the dirt, knowing Mommy's body is under there, stuffed in some box. I really hope the worms and insects don't go inside. Who will kill them for her if I'm not there to do it?

The sun rises in the sky, and I know I don't have a lot of time left. I have to get back before Emmett wakes. He asks for Mommy through the monitor every day, and when I come in the room, his bottom lip shakes until I play peekaboo with him.

Benny always asks Aunt Darla during breakfast when Mommy's coming home from heaven. She looks at Aunt Bette, and there's silence, each waiting for the other to answer. Aunt Darla's eyebrow raises the same as Mommy's when she used to ask Benny and I who started hitting who. That's when I tell Benny we're going to go outside and play football. Benny can't handle the truth. He'd cry if he knew that she's never coming back. It's my job to protect him.

Dad never comes out of his room. Aunt Darla and Aunt Bette have my cousins to take care of, and I heard Uncle Wade telling Aunt Bette the other day on the front porch that he's barely treading water taking on all the responsibilities himself. He said that somehow, they have to get Dad out of bed and to live again, otherwise we'll lose the ranch. Mommy loved the ranch, and if we lose it, I know she'd cry up in heaven.

I cross my legs and pick at the grass around the dirt.

"Mommy," I whisper.

Dead people can't talk, but everyone says she's watching over me, so she should be here. And if she's here, shouldn't I feel her? But I don't. Tears burn my eyes, but I swallow them down. I have to be strong for Benny and Emmett and Dad.

I hear a squeak, and I glance over my shoulder. Sadie shuts the gate behind her as if she's locking everyone out. I wish she could.

Her family owns the farm next door, and my mommy was

best friends with her mommy, so she's always around. She's okay, I guess. For a girl.

I don't say anything when Sadie sits by my side. She's in her white nightgown and her beat-up rain boots with ladybugs on them.

"Why are you up?" I ask, plucking another blade of grass and wrapping it around my finger.

"Daddy was loud this morning, and I saw you out here." She points at her house. Her bedroom window faces the cemetery. "Are you okay?"

"I'm fine," I say with the meanness in my voice that suddenly showed up the day my mom didn't come home.

"It's okay, you know."

I whip my head toward her. "What is?"

"To cry."

I scoff and pluck a handful of blades, tossing them one by one on the dirt pile. "I don't cry."

She sighs and crosses her legs, making sure her nightgown covers her knees. Her hands fiddle with the edge of the braid that's twisted around her head and down her neck. She's always touching her hair. "Okay."

I want to get up and leave. Leave her here and stomp back to the house. I want to be alone.

"My mommy says you're the glue."

I frown. "What does that mean?"

She shrugs. "I don't know, but glue keeps things together. Fixes things. Last year, Daddy broke Mommy's favorite vase, and he glued it back together. Couldn't even tell it'd been broken."

I roll my eyes. Sadie's mommy told my mom and my aunts that story. I'm not sure why she was always repeating that story. "Whatever."

"She said glue doesn't always stick though. And sometimes water still seeps in through the cracks. She told Daddy that one day, you won't be able to hold it together."

"I don't care, Sadie." And I don't. Her mom always says weird stuff. Saying I'm glue? Sticky white stuff that takes forever to dry? What is she even talking about?

"I think she's saying that if you don't let your feelings out, one day they'll come out anyway." Sadie's always doing this. She's so smart, and she explains things to me even when I don't need her to. "That no glue is that strong."

"Super glue is. Daddy used it on Emmett's highchair leg, and it hasn't broken since."

"Oh. Well...I don't know."

We sit in silence, listening to all the animals waking up. I need to get back.

"I miss her," Sadie says.

My hands fist the grass blades. "She wasn't your mommy."

"My mommy cries all the time. She misses her too."

Tears pool in my eyes, but I force them back. I haven't cried yet, and I'm not going to do it in front of Sadie Wilkins. "So do Benny and Emmett."

"I know. You must miss her."

A tear slips from my eye, and I swipe it away with the back of my hand.

"It's okay, Jude."

"I just have something in my eye." I rub my eyes, hoping she doesn't notice my other eye is filled with water too.

She slides closer. Her white nightgown is dirty now.

"Go home."

She wraps her arm around my shoulders. "No."

My head falls, and I can't stop the tears. They continue to run, one after the other, hitting my dirty jeans. I wipe them away with my hands, but Sadie leans over and places her head on my shoulder.

"Just go, Sadie."

"It's okay. I won't tell anyone," she whispers.

I can't stop them from coming, so I sit there and cry for the first time since Mommy died.

Chapter One

JUDE

TWENTY-SEVEN YEARS LATER...

I roll over in bed and stare at the ceiling for a bit. The roosters don't care that it's Sunday morning. It's been a long time since I've slept in anyway, so I get up and pull on my pajama pants, then tread downstairs to my kitchen. The coffee is already brewed, so I pour myself a cup and go out to my porch that overlooks the lake on Plain Daisy Ranch.

"Jesus, shirt please." Emmett, my youngest brother, walks over wearing his typical too-long basketball shorts. He lives next to me, through the line of trees, but I rarely see him on a Sunday.

"I could say the same."

"You forget, I'm still in my twenties, so..." He looks down at himself and pats his six-pack. "Yeah, I'm still perfection."

I sit in the porch chair and prop my feet up on the railing. "Why are you here?"

He pulls his phone from his shorts and holds it up. "You really need to keep your phone on you."

I like the convenience of my phone, but I could do

7

without it at times. I've never been one to keep up with social media or play mindless games on it. I'm usually the only person in a waiting room *not* on their phone.

"It's upstairs," I say.

He bounds up the porch steps and heads into my house. I roll my eyes at the banging of the cupboard and the clinking of mugs.

"Why are you here again?" I call through the screen door.

"Dad is on his way."

My forehead creases. "Why?"

He walks out with a cup of coffee, taking the other chair on the porch. The one that's barely ever sat in since I live by myself. He bounces up and down on the seat. "Cushy."

"Emmett—why?"

He stares at me for a moment. Finally remembering the question, he rocks his head back and shrugs. "Not sure. Just said to meet here in ten."

"Doesn't he have company?" I arch an eyebrow.

Sometime when we were in high school, Dad started entertaining women on Saturday nights. Sometimes they're women he picks up from a bar and brings home, but I learned years ago never to go over there on Sunday morning. Poor Ben, my other brother, is living there until his house is done, and he gives me the scoop every time my dad is making breakfast for a new woman on Sunday. I want my dad to be happy, but I don't like seeing another woman in my mom's kitchen. Not that I would tell anyone.

Emmett shrugs. "Maybe he stayed home last night."

"Doubtful." I sip my coffee.

"It's kind of sad, don't you think?"

I feel Emmett staring at me, but I don't bother turning my eyes away from the small ducks paddling around the lake. "What is?"

"That your dad has a sex life, and you don't."

"You don't know shit about my life." My lips purse.

He laughs, sips his coffee, and spits it out all over my porch.

"You're cleaning that up." I watch two ducks swimming side by side as if they're a couple.

"Why don't you just inject it through an IV right into your bloodstream?" Emmett stands. "I need milk or something."

He disappears inside again, then his clanking and banging echoes out to the porch. Likely, my kitchen will be a disaster once he's done.

I watch the ducks some more. Emmett has a point. Lately, there've been no women in my life. I don't date. I don't sleep with random women unless I'm out of town, and even that has been rare. My hand and my imagination are my Saturday night entertainment, but I'm craving one particular woman more than I'd ever admit to anyone, especially Emmett.

"Better." Emmett walks out with his cup of coffee and a banana. "I hope Dad brings breakfast."

I shake my head. It amazes me some days that Emmett manages to get dressed and out of the house on his own.

"You're kicking me out?" I hear Ben ask before he turns the corner, my dad right beside him.

Ben's holding a box and dressed in sweats and T-shirt, while my dad is wearing his usual jeans and flannel shirt unbuttoned, showing off how fit the man still is.

"You're engaged. It's time," Dad says.

Ben stops and stares at our dad, but he just continues his walk over to my steps. "Dad!"

He waves Ben off. "Go live with your family."

Ben's jaw clenches. "The house isn't ready, and you won't let me hire anyone."

Dad stops on the first step and blows out a breath. "Fine, hire people. Probably safer for Gillian and Clayton anyway."

"Mornin', Dad," Emmett says.

I'm surprised Emmett doesn't have some smart-ass comment for Ben.

Ben's gaze lands on me.

"There's no room at the inn," I say, not about to invite him to live here. Walking in on him and Gillian on my sofa is not what I need in my life right now.

"Jude. Emmett." Dad nods at us and walks into my house. Good thing my coffee maker is scheduled to make a full pot every morning.

Ben follows our dad inside and drops the box on the porch table as he walks by. "Here."

"Donuts!" Emmett acts like a five-year-old and is the first one to the box. "Who bought these?"

"Dad's...visitor made them." Ben follows my dad inside.

The two of them continue to argue about Dad kicking Ben out. We've all been there. Me at nineteen and Emmett at eighteen. He gave us the land, told us to build a house and to get out of his. But Ben just returned a few months ago after retiring from pro football, and although he catches a ball as if he's got super glue on his hands, hammering a nail into wood isn't really his skill set.

Emmett picks up a glazed donut, inspecting it. "Made them?" He shrugs and takes a big bite of one. He moans as he chews and swallows.

Dad walks out with Ben right behind him, each holding coffee mugs.

"She's a keeper." Emmett pushes the rest of the donut into his mouth.

"None of them are keepers." Dad towers over Emmett, staring down at him until Emmett gets up from the chair.

Emmett goes over to the railing, snagging another donut on his way.

Ben leans against the railing, ankles crossed, sipping his coffee.

It's been us four for the past twenty-seven years, but things are changing. Ben proposed to his high school sweetheart who has a fifteen-year-old son. Once his house is done, they'll move onto the ranch. These impromptu early morning meetings my dad calls are either going to get bigger or stop all together.

Something in my chest tightens. I'm not big on change.

"Is that what this meeting is about…you kicking me out?" Ben asks. He's never been a morning guy, and I'm sure he got used to his cushy life in San Francisco.

"You gotta try one." Emmett holds up his half-eaten donut in front of Ben.

Ben rears back. "If I want one, I'll grab one. I don't need one you had your mouth all over."

"You act like I have cooties. We're not five." Emmett finishes his second donut with a pout.

I think Ben and I both forget how sensitive Emmett is. Sure, he deflects it with humor, but I'm sure the fact that Gillian will be joining our family feels weird to him too. He doesn't remember Mom. Then again, sometimes I feel guilty at the end of a long day when she hasn't crossed my mind.

"You sure about that?" Ben asks.

Emmett places his coffee on the railing, storming toward Ben.

"Enough," Dad says, pulling his attention from the lake in front of us. "Ben, you have a family now, which means you need to fly from the nest."

As usual, my dad's tone leaves no room for argument.

Ben scoffs.

"But that isn't what this is about. Last night, I heard something. I have some news." Dad sips his coffee, puts it on the table between us, and rests his forearms on his legs.

"Are you getting married?" Emmett asks, grabbing two donuts at once.

"Fuck off, Emmett," I say.

Dad doesn't say anything, burying his head in his cup of coffee again.

"I'm just saying...if I can get donuts like this every morning..." Emmett licks his fingers one at a time.

"It's about the Wilkins's ranch."

My feet fall to the porch, and I sit up in my chair. Something about the tone of his voice makes me tense. "What about it?"

"Calm down, cowboy." Emmett chuckles.

Ben punches Emmett in the arm.

"Ouch. Fuck. Damn it, that hurt." He goes to punch Ben, but Ben dodges him, and the two weave around one another, coffee spilling on my porch.

"Enough." Dad eyes both of them.

Ben gets one more playful slap on Emmett's cheek, and they separate.

"You two finished?" Dad asks, and my brothers sober. "We all know the flood a few years back wasn't good for their land. I thought things were improving, Monty got a crop of soybeans last year, but rumor is they're behind on payments."

"What are you saying?" I broach the real question at hand.

"They might lose the ranch." He leans back in his chair, resting his ankle over his knee, picking up his coffee mug.

"Fuck," Emmett says.

"Sadie ever say anything?" Ben asks me.

I shake my head. My best friend might not know anything. Her dad is old-school, and since Mr. and Mrs. Wilkins couldn't have kids after Sadie, he never had a son to take over the ranch like so many others in our area have done over the years. Shit, my dad hit the jackpot with us three, although being the eldest means most of the responsibility has landed on me.

"Did you hear how bad it is?" Emmett asks.

My brothers are concerned. I can tell by their expressions. No one in our area wants to see a family ranch get taken by the bank. Land has been passed down for generations around here, and there are always vultures waiting to swoop in and steal it away.

I worry for Mr. and Mrs. Wilkins, but it's Sadie who's at the forefront of my mind. She would have helped her family, but if she's been kept in the dark, it might just be too late. Everyone knows how prideful ranchers are about their land. My dad went through hell after Mom died, and if it wasn't for people stepping up, we probably would have lost our ranch.

I stand. "I have to call Sadie."

"If you'd keep your phone on you, you wouldn't have to walk up those stairs," Emmett says.

I push Emmett in the chest, and he exaggerates it, flipping over the porch railing, landing on his feet on the grass below.

"You're a dumbass," Ben says and takes my seat next to Dad.

"Just wait," my dad says.

I stop with my hand on the screen door. "I want to—"

"I called you all here because if the rumors are true, I plan on taking it over."

"What?" my brothers and I ask in unison.

He shakes his head. "I didn't say buy it. I'm going to help Monty bring the ranch back to life, but it's gonna take me away from our ranch."

I reluctantly nod. It's the right thing to do, but that means my workload just increased two times.

"It's the least I can do to repay him for what he did for us after Mom..." Dad gulps. "This is a good time to get Emmett up to speed. You've taken a lot on, Jude. Time to train him so he can take some things from you."

"Do I get a raise?" Emmett jumps back up on the porch.

No one answers him.

I know enough to know that this isn't up for discussion. Not that I'd argue. The success of the Wilkins farm has a direct correlation to Sadie's happiness. It's bad enough that she had to stay here after high school. She should've been long gone from Willowbrook by now. Deserves to be.

"We're agreed?" Dad looks at each one of us, and we nod. "Now, Ben, go pack up your shit and get out." Dad stands and puts on his cowboy hat, stepping off the porch without another word.

Ben grumbles and follows him while Emmett stares at the box of donuts then back at me.

"Just take them." I grab all the coffee mugs and go back into my house.

"See you tomorrow, Bossman!" Emmett calls as he leaves.

I blow out a breath. After dropping the mugs in the sink, I take the stairs two at a time. I swipe my phone off the nightstand and sit on the edge of my bed.

I press my finger to the screen and find a text from Sadie.

> Morning. Want to do lunch? I have
> something to talk to you about.

Maybe she does know.

> Definitely. I'll pick you up at noon.

Although she sent the text a half hour ago, the three dots appear as if she was waiting for me to answer.

> Great. See you then.

A million ways to solve this problem for her run through my mind because there's nothing I hate more than seeing Sadie upset.

Chapter Two

"So, why the early Sunday morning meet-up?" Lottie asks once she's finished complaining about her hangover. She's on the opposite side of the booth and resting her head on the vinyl back as if she's going to take a nap.

I raise my chin, suck in a breath, and proclaim, "I've decided it's time."

Her back straightens. She looks around at the half-filled booths in the Easy Eggs Diner and leans forward. We're just off the highway, and some people might recognize us, but most of the customers here are people traveling through. "For real?"

I nod, biting down on my smile.

"Miss!" Lottie waves at the waitress passing by. "We're going to need some mimosas."

The waitress raises both eyebrows. "The best I got is vodka from my flask I can put into your orange juice." She starts to walk away.

"Pancakes with whipped cream?" Lottie smiles wide.

The waitress stops but doesn't turn around. "I'll add chocolate chips."

"Perfect." She turns back to me. "We'll celebrate with champagne after you tell my cousin how you feel, and he confesses his undying love for you."

"Let's not get ahead of ourselves." I slip my chai tea bag into my cup so it can steep.

"Oh, stop it. The two of you have loved each other forever."

She's wrong about that. I'm not sure how Jude views me. Sure, I'm his best friend, but there have been times I swear I've caught him looking at me. But he's never crossed the line. Ever.

"So, what gives?" Lottie perks up from her earlier complaints about a hangover.

"What?"

"Why now?"

I shrug. "There wasn't really a catalyst per se. I was over there last night—we've been bingeing this crime show—and he drove me home. The moon was full, and the stars were out. He dropped me off on my porch, and we stood there for a moment. Something passed between us, I know it did. But then he stuffed his hands into his pockets and left."

"And?" I hate how well Lottie knows me.

"I went up to my old bedroom and saw him stop at his mom's gravesite."

She slaps the table. "I knew it." A few people turn and look at us, and she holds up her hand. "Sorry. We just have some exciting news over here."

A few old men grumble, turning back to their conversations—most likely about the land and their crops and harvest time.

"Continue."

I sip my tea. "That's it. He stopped and talked to his mom like I've seen him do a thousand times. Then he got up and disappeared into the darkness."

The waitress is a welcome distraction when she places the pancakes with whipped cream and chocolate chips on them in front of us. There's even a sliced strawberry for a nose. It looks delicious.

"Can I actually have two egg whites with spinach and parmesan cheese? And a side of fruit?" I ask with a grimace.

"So she's the only one celebrating?" The waitress's expression says that she'd rather have her legs in stirrups for her annual exam than be here serving us.

"She's just a pessimist," Lottie says over a mouthful of pancake.

The woman walks away without a word. Jeez, she's grumpier than Jude can be.

I look back at Lottie. "I'm a realist, there's a difference."

She swallows her pancake, pushing the plate away. "Carbs are too addictive. That's my limit."

"You took one bite."

"Miss Egg-Whites-and-Spinach should understand."

I nod and laugh. "Maybe I shouldn't do it," I say, my nerves getting the best of me.

"Not tell Jude?" She forks another bite of pancake, unable to help herself.

"If he doesn't feel the same way, it'll change our dynamic. I should wait until after we finish bingeing the crime show at least."

The pancake rests on the edge of her fork, and her eyes drill into mine for a second, then two, then three.

I squirm under her scrutiny. "I get it. I just really want to know what happened to the girl on the show, and if he turns me down, I won't be able to watch it. We don't have that streaming platform at my little cottage."

She puts the delicious-looking pancake in her mouth, still saying nothing until she swallows. "If he doesn't see what's right in front of him after all these years, it's about time you move on. I mean..."

Here we go. The same talk everyone gives me. I can't wait around for Jude Noughton forever.

"Eventually, you have to move—"

"I know!" I say too loudly and lower my voice. "I know. I do. But it's like I don't see other guys."

"Really? No one else?"

"Well, I mean, sure, models and actors, but no one local. There's no one else." With my eyes, I will her to understand.

"Well, if this goes south, we're going to Lincoln. You'll find a great rebound there."

"Is it technically a rebound if he was never mine?" I tilt my head.

The waitress comes back over and puts my plate of food in front of me. My stomach grumbles. I thank her, and she gives me a soft smile before helping the people two tables down.

"Let's put this plan in motion. Today is the day."

"Today?" My eyebrows raise. "It's Sunday."

She swipes a blueberry from my cup and pops it in her mouth. "What were you going to do? Meet him on the ranch tomorrow while he's got his hands on Bessie's udders and say, 'why don't you touch mine?'"

I cringe. "Gross. And he doesn't milk Bessie."

She laughs. "Get that phone out and text him."

I set my fork down and reach into my purse, my thumb hovering over his name on the screen.

"Calm that racing heart. You're just asking him to meet up," Lottie says.

I nod, giving myself a small mental pep talk that there's a reason I asked Lottie to meet me for breakfast this morning. And there's a reason why something shifted last night and told me now is the time. I know I'm not alone in this. I know the guy well enough, so I need to stop freaking out.

Then again, what if he doesn't feel the same as me? I can't imagine not having him in my life. And let's be honest, if he doesn't feel the same way, Jude will retreat, and I might never get him to open up to me.

"Give me the phone." She puts her hand out over the table.

I grip it tighter and shake my head. "I can do it."

"Okay then." She forks more pancake.

Any other day, I'd call her out like she always tells me to because as she puts it "she's her own worst enemy," but she was a good friend this morning when I woke her up and said we had to meet.

I hammer out the text quickly before I lose my nerve.

> Morning. Want to do lunch? I have
> something to talk to you about.

I wait for a few seconds. No answer. Great.

"Maybe he's not awake," Lottie says with her coffee cup in the air, waiting for the waitress to refill her.

"This is Jude. He wakes up with the roosters."

"If you were in bed with him, he wouldn't." She waggles her eyebrows.

"Let's just talk about something else." I put my phone in my purse and bury my head in my plate.

"Sadie?" Lottie asks a minute later when neither of us has said anything else. I lift up my head, and Lottie studies me for a beat. "He'd be a fool not to return your affections. You know that, right? You're the best thing in his life, and if he can't see that, he's a fool, even if he's my cousin."

I smile, my body calming. I wasn't even aware how much I needed to hear those words, but I know in my gut that Jude and I are at a crossroads. It's time to either move on hand in hand or part ways. The thought of seeing him with a woman, a wife, who isn't me, feels like someone is holding a knife to my throat. But it's now or never.

"Thank you."

She places her hand over mine and squeezes without saying anything sarcastic. She's been a great friend to me over the years, and I'm lucky to have her as a sounding board.

We finish our breakfast and hug goodbye in the parking lot. When I get into my car, my phone dings with a text message from Jude.

> Definitely. I'll pick you up at noon.

All the nerves I managed to settle in the diner double. I remind myself that Lottie is right, he'd be a fool, so I respond.

> Great. See you then.

&.

I SHOOT HOME TO SHOWER, SHAVE, AND DO MY HAIR and makeup just to make sure I look my best. Not that Jude is one to notice or say anything about my appearance, but if I'm going to finally put myself out there after all these years, I'm going to get prettied up.

I pass Jude's family ranch and turn down the dirt road to ours. We don't have the iron arch, and our fence isn't newly painted like theirs. A flood a few years back devastated our acreage, which is a small amount compared to most people around here. But this year was the first year since then that I think we turned a profit. I wouldn't know, since my dad is too prideful to tell me anything. Even after I ended up staying here after high school instead of going to college, he doesn't want me to be part of the company financials.

I park in front of our house that my dad has had no time

to keep up. The red paint peels off the shutters, and the wooden porch stairs are worn from never being freshened up. My dad's truck is in front of the house, which is unusual since Sundays aren't restful for my dad anymore. He works our farm seven days a week.

Although I've moved into the small one-room cottage behind my parents' house that they built for my grandma, I always check on Mom as soon as I get home.

I climb the porch stairs, checking my watch and seeing I have two hours to get ready.

I continue to give myself the pep talk I need to spit out the words to Jude in a little bit. There have been signs with Jude over the years—small ones—but I never know if it's friendship or more. Even though he's my best friend, he's so damn hard to read.

A scream echoes out of the house, freezing me in place.

Mom.

Oh shit, I hope she didn't fall again.

My footsteps pound on the uneven porch boards, and I rush through the front screen door, following my mom's yells. "Mom!"

"In here. Oh, Sadie. Help!"

Panic flares as I fly up the stairs, pumping my arms. My mom cries out for me again. Please tell me this isn't the day I've feared since high school graduation. She's been better lately, the new medication helping her symptoms.

I run through my parents' bedroom door and find my mom's hands on my dad's chest.

"Mom?" It takes my brain a minute to make sense of what I'm seeing. It's not my mom in trouble, it's my dad.

She looks at me with tears streaming down her cheeks, and she doesn't have to say a word for me to know it's likely too late. "Call the ambulance."

Her voice is too calm, and her nursing hands aren't nearly

as strong as they once were as she pushes down on my dad's chest, his lifeless body not responding. I pull my phone out of my purse, dial 911, and walk out of the room, still in shock.

After telling them everything, I rush back to the bedroom, and everything slows. My mom takes control of the situation, instructing me to check for a pulse and breathing. She works on my dad until she's too tired, and her hands cramp.

Then she looks up at me, bewildered. "I don't think...I got to him too late. He went up for a nap after breakfast, said he wasn't feeling well, and I came to check on him."

Sirens ring through the open windows, and I leave my mom to meet the paramedics. The ambulance pulls down our dirt road, and I sit on the porch steps, leaning my head on the railing. They park behind my car, and I stand, walking down the steps as they round the back, coming into view with a stretcher.

One paramedic, Teri, a girl I went to school with, sees the expression on my face, and I shake my head. It's too late, he's gone, but I can't form the words. They leave the stretcher at the bottom of the porch steps.

"Second bedroom on your left," I say.

Teri and her partner head in the direction I point, and the porch steps creak as I fall back down to sit.

"Sadie!"

Jude's voice draws my attention, and I look around, finding him riding Titan my way. Once he's close, he slows Titan, swings one leg over the horse, and drops onto the ground. I run into his arms, and he swallows me up in his big body.

"I saw the ambulance pass the house. Is your mom okay?"

I shake my head against his chest. "It's Dad. He's dead."

His arms grip tighter, and I welcome the safety that only he can provide me.

Chapter Three

JUDE

The ambulance pulls down the drive without the lights flashing, and Sadie's dad's body is in the back. My dad came over as soon as I texted. He's inside with Sadie's mom while I hold Sadie to my side.

"I'm so sorry," I say.

She slides away from me and walks to the edge of the porch where the best view of their farmland is. "What am I going to do?"

I stand at her side. Their farm isn't producing as it should. It's had years of neglect I'm not sure can be reversed. But they got something going this year. Not their entire property, but part. "I'll help. My dad will. Everyone will pitch in and get it going."

She sighs and leans her head on the post of the railing, wrapping her arm around it. "Even if we get it going, Jude, I can't keep it running. I'd have to hire a bunch of workers, and I have no clue if we can afford that."

I have my theories as to why her dad was so close to his vest about the farm going under. Sadie's a fixer. She's a "tell me the problem, and I'll map my way through it" girl. Which is an admirable quality—hell, it's what's going to get her through what she's dealing with now. But I'm sure Monty Wilkins didn't want his daughter feeling the pressure of keeping a farm in the black.

She came to me crying once because her dad told her the farm was her husband's. That whoever she married, he'd sign it over to him and not her. He was incredibly old-school. And look where his close-mindedness got him—a wife and daughter left unprepared to fill his shoes.

"You could sell?" I say, knowing she's not going to like that suggestion.

"Absolutely not. This is my family's land, my ancestors' land. I know it's small, but it's ours. My dad would hate the idea of that."

I cross my arms and widen my stance. I get her point. Plain Daisy Ranch was Noughton Farm before my mom died, and my dad changed the name to honor my mom, Daisy. But some people still refer to it as Noughton Farm because it's our family land and that means something around here.

"Then we'll figure it out. I'll help."

I have no idea how I'll do it all, but for Sadie, I'll figure it out. She deserves a life filled with so much more than she has. She should've been like Ben and gotten out of here after high school, gone off to live her dreams, but she took on the responsibility of her mom's health so her dad could continue to run the farm. She's filled her time with trying to prove to her dad that she can manage the farm. Doing their website, artwork that he never wanted, suggestions on how to build a brand for their name. But he stood in her way, one suggestion after the other.

"How are you going to do that, Jude? You have your own ranch to look after." Her eyes haven't left the acreage in front of us. The field has to be harvested soon, which means there isn't any time for us to come up with a plan.

I weave my arm around her waist. "I'll make time."

I don't want to mention what my dad heard last night. It will only embarrass Sadie that the town knows about her dad's debts.

"Jude," my dad calls from inside the screen door.

I turn away from Sadie and walk down the half-rotted wooden planks. My dad is holding a piece of paper. He pushes open the screen, and I walk in, seeing a stack of papers in front of her mom at their dining room table.

"What's going on?" I frown.

My dad hands me a piece of paper with Notice of Default written in big black lettering across the top. I blow out a breath and look at my dad. He shows no emotion, and I'm sure that's for Mrs. Wilkins's benefit.

"Sadie?" I call.

I'm not sure this is the best idea right now, but I'm not going to keep this from her. Even if she knows the farm is in financial straits, this is another level entirely. If her mom thought it was important enough to tell my dad, then Sadie needs to know.

Her footsteps along the porch vibrate the floorboards, and I worry one day that this house might crumble to the ground.

"What's going on?" She looks at my hands, the paper, then her eyes close. I fucking hate making her upset. Her eyes open and zero in on her mom. "Really?"

"He thought he'd have time. That the harvest would save us." Rhea Wilkins is a loving mother, but after she was diagnosed with an autoimmune disease that seems to have snowballed into one issue after another over the last decade, she hasn't been able to do much on the farm. Which is why Sadie stayed back at eighteen.

"You kept it from me?" Sadie tears the sheet of paper from my hands. "Notice of Default?" Her eyes scan the paper, and her mouth hangs open. "Mom, this letter is from over a month ago!"

"Your dad was talking to the bank, but..." Her chin falls to her chest, and I want to step in front of Sadie to shield her from the shitty news that's about to come out of her mom.

Instead of telling Sadie whatever she was going to, her shoulders shake, and a quiet sob flows out of her.

Sadie crosses the room and squats next to her mom, putting her arm around her. "Don't cry. What is it?"

My dad side-eyes me, and I prepare myself for worse news. He bends down, picking up the newspaper from this morning that's folded over twice. He hands it over to me, pointing at the Notice of Sale. My heart sinks, and my dad nods.

"Sadie," I say, voice hoarse.

She looks at me, and her gaze goes to the paper in my hands. Maybe I shouldn't be so forthcoming, allow Sadie to grieve before she finds out that she might lose everything today, but I promised her a long time ago I'd never hide anything from her. I already hide one thing from her every time we're together, but that's for both our sakes.

"It's a Notice of Sale," I say, lifting the newspaper.

"You might have six weeks to get current on payments," my dad adds.

She stands and looks at the papers stacked in front of her mom. "Why would you guys keep all this from me?"

Her mom wipes her eyes, and my dad grabs a tissue box from the living room, placing it in front of Rhea. "You know your dad."

Sadie takes the papers and sits down. "All of these are letters from the mortgage company, loans for equipment." Her fingers breeze through them. "I can't believe you kept this from me."

Dad touches my arm and nods toward the door, but my

feet don't move. I can't leave her here to deal with this on her own.

After clearing his throat, my dad says, "We'll just step outside," giving me a look.

I don't want to go. Sadie's face grows redder and redder, and I know she's going to lose it soon. I need to be here for her. But I know my dad, and I have to think of how this is going to work. This entails more than my dad coming to help on the farm this harvest season.

"I'll just be on the porch, Sadie," I say.

But she's not paying me any mind, asking her mom questions that Rhea can't answer except for "you know your father."

Once the screen door shuts, my dad walks to the end of the porch where Sadie stood moments ago, looking out at their land. He shoves his hands in his pockets. I follow and stand next to him.

He huffs. "It's not looking good. I mean, even if we were to try to buy it for Rhea and Sadie, I'm not sure…"

My dad isn't a man who gives up easily. The only time I've ever seen or heard pessimistic words or actions out of him was after Mom died.

"I'll work extra here, after I'm done at the ranch."

He side-eyes me. "I know you want to do it for Sadie, but at this point"—he glances over his shoulder—"they might be better off to just let it go."

"Dad—"

"I know. I know." He studies the land again, deep in thought. "Let's call Ben and Gillian. She's the lawyer in the family now. We'll go from there."

I pull out my phone, walking down the porch and peeking through the screen door to check in on Sadie, who has her hand over her mom's. I dial my middle brother, thankful he's marrying the next town lawyer. Sure, Gillian hasn't made any final decisions about staying in Willowbrook, but for now, she's finishing up her articling phase in town. She might have wanted out of this town once, but now with Ben's return and Clayton in high school, she'll stay.

The call goes to Ben's voicemail the first time, so I call again.

"What's up?" Ben answers, sounding irritated.

"Hey...um, I know you're at Gillian's, but I have some news. Sadie's dad just died." He doesn't say anything, so I continue. "And if you read the paper today, a Notice of Sale was printed. The farm's been in default for months."

"Okay, we'll be right there." Ben isn't going to ask questions. He's aware of the severity.

"Thanks."

We hang up, and I shove my phone back in my pocket, going over to Titan while wishing I would have driven my truck. I run my hand down his mane.

"Call Emmett, tell him to come get Titan," my dad says.

I'm not sure if it's from living with only men the majority of our lives, but it's as if we can all read each other's thoughts.

I call Emmett and tell him the news and to keep his mouth shut. Although my younger brother knows when to not spread gossip that could hurt people, especially the Wilkins. They've been our neighbors all our lives and helped us numerous times through the years.

When I hang up, my dad sets his hands on his hips and says to me, "We just have to get them through the burial, then we'll worry about the farm."

"I'm not sure—"

"Rhea lost her husband. Sadie lost her father. That trumps anything to do with the farm."

I nod, but I can't help the part of me that wants to get their farm ready for harvest and figure out the parts that haven't been able to produce for them since the flood.

Sadie walks out of the house but doesn't walk toward me. Instead she heads down the porch steps and rounds the wrap-around porch, heading behind the house, most likely to her place.

My dad nods in her direction. "Go. I'll be with Rhea, and hopefully when Ben and Gillian get here, we can sit down." He walks across the front lawn, and I follow Sadie.

Hopefully Emmett will be here soon to ride Titan back.

"Sadie," I say, approaching her.

She ignores me and walks inside her small cottage, the one her grandma lived in when we were younger. That woman baked the best snickerdoodle cookies. I don't knock, opening the door and walking in. She's sitting on the edge of her couch, staring at her hands.

"I don't understand. I'm not sure I could've fixed it, but why didn't he trust me enough to tell me what was going on?" She doesn't look up at me.

The old couch dips as I sit next to her. "I'm not sure there's anything you could've done."

I don't mean for my words to be harsh, but Sadie was always kept from farm life. She can't drive the equipment. She spends the majority of her time at her desk or in her own small garden.

She sits up straighter. "Gee, thanks, Jude."

Fuck. Maybe I'm the wrong person to be consoling her. She needs a woman.

"Want me to call Lottie?"

"Jesus, Jude." She stands, retreating from me, but the space is small. Clean and tidy and homey, but small. It's why we always hang at my place. "I thought you were different from them." She points in the direction of the fields, insinuating that the farmers all think of her as her dad did.

"I'm not saying that. It's just...it's not your fault that your dad never allowed you to help."

"I can do it, and I'm going to. Just watch me." She storms out of the cottage.

My chin falls to my chest.

This is the reason I can't ever be in a serious relationship with anyone. I don't have comforting instincts like Ben. The ones where you know how to help a woman and console her. I just seem to fuck it up whenever I open my mouth.

Chapter Four

JUDE

Monty Wilkins's funeral was a packed house. We all went to the cemetery, buried him next to his parents, then everyone in town followed us to my family home.

Of course, my dad volunteered to host the reception, and my cousin Jensen is catering the entire event that my other cousin Romy decorated perfectly. Everyone's huddled into groups with their drinks and food, telling stories about Monty. Some funny, some quirky, but most are just about what a good guy he was. I wish I wasn't so angry with the man who was like an uncle to me.

I stand off to the side of the groups, my attention only on Sadie. She's barely talked to me since she walked out on me the other day. I'm not doubting her ability. She's got a work ethic I'm fucking jealous of, and I work from sunup to sundown during certain times of the year. I probably shouldn't have shot her down so fast. It was a knee-jerk reaction on my part, and she hadn't even processed the death of her father.

"Jude Noughton, always looking so deep in thought." My cousin Lottie, who is also Sadie's best friend, sidles up beside me. I don't feel like dealing with her while Sadie is pissed at me.

"Lottie." I tip my beer back, needing more alcohol before she speaks.

I love Lottie. She's my cousin and definitely team Sadie against anyone who wrongs her, but she's got opinions I don't always agree with.

"Why are you saying my name with such disdain today?"

Both of us look at Sadie huddled with Mrs. Fortmeyer and a few of the other women who are involved in every chili cook-off, bake sale, and whatever else this town puts on. They're nice but gossipy.

"Always watching her." Lottie clucks her tongue.

I side-eye her. "You make me sound like a creep."

"Well, you do have that whole strong, silent, grumpy thing going on that some people might construe as creepy." I glare at her, and she holds up her hands. "You know, if they didn't know you."

I huff and down the rest of my beer.

"Case in point," she says.

We watch the crowd in silence, and I wait for her to leave me alone.

"She's going to crack."

Guess she's not going anywhere.

"I know," I say.

"She can only put up this strong front for so long."

"I know."

"Are you going to catch her?"

"What do you think?" I stare longingly at the beer area, wishing I had a fresh one.

"I think you'll go into fix-it mode and forget that she needs nurturing too."

"Lottie Dotty." Emmett joins us and hands me a beer. Thank fuck for his interruption.

"How's it going, little cuz?" Lottie says with a grin.

Emmett's lips straighten. He absolutely hates that nickname, and rarely do people call him that now unless they're trying to piss him off. "If you weren't my cousin, I'd take you behind the barn and show you just how *not* little I am."

Her nose wrinkles. "Gross. I've had my fill of your kind."

I step back, hoping the two of them will go after one another so I can disappear.

"Good-looking, strong, and an exceptional fuck you mean?"

Lottie bursts out laughing, bending over. "Shit. One day you're gonna come across some woman who will give it back as good."

Emmett tips back his beer. "Looking forward to it. Maybe I'll lock her down."

Lottie rolls her eyes. "Emmett Noughton, a one-woman man? Right, can't wait to see that."

Emmett hits me with his elbow. "Ah, come on, Jude here is about to lose his bachelor card. There's hope for me yet."

Lottie's head whips in my direction so fast, a stiff breeze blows against my face. "What?"

Emmett laughs. "You'd think she was the one in love with you."

Lottie holds her hand up to Emmett. "Jude, what's he talking about?"

Does Lottie really believe if I was with someone, everyone in this town wouldn't know it? It would be on The Canary Post down at The Hidden Cave in five minutes.

I scowl at her. "He doesn't know what the hell he's talking about."

Her body visibly relaxes. "So you're not dating anyone?"

"I'm sure you'd know if I was."

Lottie's eyes narrow on Emmett as if asking him if I'm not being truthful.

Right then, Sadie looks around the crowd. Our eyes lock for a moment before she turns back to the older woman.

"Jude only loves one woman, and I have a bet going," Emmett says.

"A bet?" I look at him.

"Oh, do tell." Lottie steps closer, leaning forward.

"If I tell you in front of Jude, he might purposely make it so I lose."

Lottie glances at me.

I shake my head in exasperation. "I don't really care about your stupid fucking bet, Emmett."

He nods to the side, and the two of them go under the oak tree I planted on Earth Day when I was seven. I know what the bet has to do with without even having to ask Emmett. I'm sure it involves Ben, and I'm also sure it involves something to do with Sadie and me. But I don't give a shit what they're saying. Never have.

Sadie politely steps away from the women and weaves through the crowd, not stopping to talk to the people stepping in front of her to offer their condolences. She heads into the house I grew up in, and I dump my half-drank beer, following her inside.

She's at the kitchen table with her head in her hands, her back racking with sobs.

"Are you okay?" I ask, folding myself into the chair next to her. I want to touch her, but I don't think she wants me to.

"I just need a minute," Sadie says. "Everyone's asking all these questions and judging my dad."

"Screw 'em."

I've heard the bastards, too, and I can't say that judgments haven't been running through my mind, although I'd never speak them. I understand Monty's pride, and I'm sure he didn't think a heart attack was coming for him, but at some point, pride needs to be put aside. He should have thought of

Rhea and Sadie. Sadie gave up her entire life for Rhea and the farm, and this is how she's rewarded.

"What am I going to do? I'll never get that much money in two months."

After the Notice of Sale was put on the Wilkins's farm, Gillian helped Sadie look into everything, and it turns out her dad hadn't paid the mortgage in almost an entire year. He made promises to the bank that he never made good on. Now, they've filed a Notice of Sale which only gives her two months to pay back a year's worth of mortgage payments. Otherwise, the farm goes up for sale. It's an impossible situation.

"I'll help you. You aren't alone."

A sob rips from Sadie, and my chest squeezes. My heart aches to take her pain away.

"What are you going to do, Jude? The land is crap after that flood. I should've known. We never recovered after that."

"This isn't the time to discuss this." I put my hand on her forearm.

"When is the time?" The chair legs screech against the floor as she bolts up to standing. "Forget it. I just want this day to be over."

She leaves me at the kitchen table, and the back screen door bangs against the wooden frame. I blow out a breath and lean back in my chair.

"Gill!" Ben shouts through the front screen door.

I turn and look through the archway into our family room.

"Shh..." a woman who I'm pretty sure is Gillian says.

"Why are you hiding in the family room?" Ben asks.

You've got to be kidding me? Gillian was listening to all that?

I get up from the chair and round the corner to find Gillian biting the corner of her lip, guilt all over her face. "You eavesdropping, Gill?"

"I didn't want to interrupt."

Ben walks through the screen door.

I crack my neck, and it pops. I don't remember the last time I was this stressed.

"How is she?" Ben asks.

"How do you think?" What a stupid-ass question. He was young, but he has to remember the feeling he had when we lost Mom. Add in the fact that the future of her family's land is on her shoulders now.

Ben doesn't argue with me.

"Two months to find that kind of money..." I shake my head.

There are very few options. Fundraisers would never raise enough. Harvest isn't going to turn a big enough profit. I'm not sure what Sadie's thinking, but everything in farming takes time, and that's the one thing we don't have on our side.

"I was thinking," Ben says.

He better not say what I think he's about to say. Before he can even suggest being the fucking hero, I shoot him down. "No."

"It could be a loan. She can pay us back whenever." I think it's great that my little brother has millions in the bank. Good for him and good for Gillian when she marries him because I know Ben, and he'd never make her sign a prenup. But there's zero chance I'm going to let him do this.

"No." I repeat myself.

"It's the only solution. Let us help," he says.

Gillian withdraws from our little circle. She's obviously not comfortable with this conversation. I'm sure no matter what Ben says, Gillian still believes that it's Ben's money, not hers. Allowing Ben to cut a check would be the easy fix, but his money isn't welcome here. He's not the white knight in this story.

"Sadie is mine," I say without running those words through my head first.

Ben raises his eyebrows with a smirk that makes me want to drop-kick him to the floor and wrestle it off his face.

"You know what I fucking meant. She's my best friend."

"But that's not what you said." Ben chuckles.

Gillian sighs, rolling her eyes, fully aware we might throw down in the middle of a funeral.

Years ago, this would've turned into a fight that would probably end up with Dad pulling one of us off the other, but I won't add more stress to Sadie's life right now.

"Fuck off, Ben. You're not going to be the hero and save the day." I turn on my heel and stalk back to the kitchen.

"Because you want to be Sadie's hero?" Ben calls after me.

I hear his laughter ringing as the back screen door slams shut behind me. Fuck him, but I'll never tell him how right he is. I'll do whatever it takes to help Sadie out of this shit situation.

Chapter Five

SADIE

I'm not sure how to start the process of making my family farm profitable. Now that we've buried my dad, I need to figure it out. My mom is deep in her grief, so I check on her extra, but she seems to want her space. The last thing I want to do is stress her out by talking about where we'll live if we lose the farm.

I have to keep my eye on the prize here. I have to set aside the devastation of losing my dad and figure out how to save this farm. There will be time for mourning later. We're almost down to seven weeks for me to get this debt paid off. Which is why I'm getting ready to head over to the bank.

I step out of the shower and dry myself off, going over in my head my plan for the land and how to secure a loan from the bank.

"Sadie!" Jude shouts, and I hear him walk into my small cottage.

Any other day, it wouldn't be a big deal, but I'm still mad at him for doubting my ability to do something to help this farm. I get his point—he's been the go-to guy at Plain Daisy Ranch for more than a decade, and I can't exactly harvest the

41

soybeans myself—but had my dad listened to me, I wouldn't be on my way to the bank.

I wrap a towel around myself, and steam rushes out the bathroom door when I open it. "Give me a second," I say, but he's there standing in the entry of the small hallway from my living quarters that leads to my bathroom and bedroom.

"Oh." He shoves his hands into his pockets and shifts his weight. "It's noon, I figured you were done with..." He pulls one hand out of his pocket and motions to me. "That."

"Showering?"

He gulps and turns his gaze away from me. "Yeah."

A part of me likes that he's uncomfortable that I'm naked under this towel, although Jude is as complicated as the exceptional corn maze he plows every October. I have no idea if his discomfort is just because I'm his best friend, and he's trying to be respectful, or if it bothers him because he's attracted to me.

"Why are you here, Jude?"

"I wanted to apologize."

I scoff and head to my room, needing space. I shouldn't want him to be antsy around me because I'm naked. I shouldn't want him to tear the towel off my body, pick me up, and toss me on my bed. Especially the way he's all dirty from the farm in his worn-in jeans covered in dirt with even some smeared on his face. He must be coming over during his lunch instead of eating with the rest of the crew.

I give my head a shake. I have bigger things to worry about right now than whether Jude finds me attractive.

He remains in the small hallway. "Don't give me the silent treatment."

I peek my head out of my room. "I'm not."

"Then you accept my apology?"

"How apologetic are you?" I shout now that I'm in my bra

and panties, changing into a sundress that will hopefully let the bank see me as a woman they need to invest in.

"I'm here, aren't I? C'mon, Sadie."

I slide the dress over my body, my hair wrapped in a towel still. "Zip me up, and you're forgiven." I walk out of the room, holding the back of my dress tight with my fist, and turn my back to him. "Jude?" I say when he still hasn't zipped up my dress after a moment.

"Yeah." He croaks, and one finger touches the small of my back, igniting a rush of goose bumps to spread on my bare skin as he slides up the zipper. "There."

"Thanks." I take the towel from my hair, scrunching my blonde curls.

"Where are you going?" He leans against the wall across from the bathroom as I continue getting ready in front of the mirror.

I'm not so sure I want to tell him, but the way this town is, he'll find out anyway.

"The bank." I put curl cream into my palm and run it through my hands before applying it to my hair.

"The bank?" His forehead wrinkles.

I glance over, and god, he looks so sexy. His legs are crossed at the ankles, his arms crossed over his chest, and his brown eyes are on me. What I wouldn't do for him to be mine and be able to walk over to him right now and ask him to take me to bed. It feels like a lifetime ago that I was ready to pour my heart out to him, but then my dad died, and I can't deal with the possibility of a fallout right now. It's the one thing that I *can* put on the back burner. I mean, my attraction to him has been there forever anyway—it can wait a few months.

I look back at myself in the mirror. "That's what I said."

"Why?"

I stop scrunching my hair, stand up straight, and glare at

him. "Why did you come here to apologize if you still think I can't handle this myself?"

He holds up both hands. "I didn't say that. I just don't think the bank is going to do much."

"It doesn't hurt to ask."

He remains quiet, and I know what he's thinking. Why would I bother going when I don't have anything to offer them for the loan? The Wilkins name doesn't mean a lot, but I have to try. It's my only hope.

"True." He uses that tone he does when he doesn't want to argue with me. Like when we watch a who-done-it, and we disagree. As if he's silently going to wait until I have no choice but to tell him he was right. Which really makes me wish I had some fairy godmother to grant me a pile of money just to stick it to him.

"I get it, okay? I have nothing. They're probably going to shoot me down, but I have to at least try. I'm out of options here."

He raises his hands over the doorframe, his body swaying into my already cramped space. Why is it so hot when guys stand like that? "You have me."

I should turn to open my makeup drawer, but before I do, I glimpse at the small amount of his stomach revealed with his shirt riding up, the light sprinkle of dark hair running down under his worn belt buckle. Is he trying to kill me?

"Sadie," he says my name so softly it flows like sweet honey down my body.

I look up, and his gaze is on me. I swallow past the dryness in my throat.

"You always have me," he repeats.

My heart flutters like a new butterfly just out of its cocoon. "I know."

"Do you?" He leans in, the muscles in his arms flexing to hold his body in place.

"Yes." I don't voice all the questions that run rampant in my brain all the time, like how much of him will I always have, what happens if he meets some woman tomorrow who he falls head over heels for? Who will I be to him then?

"Good. I gotta head back, but call me if you need me." He pushes himself back, and I immediately miss his scent. "Good luck at the bank."

"Do you really mean that?"

He chuckles and shakes his head. "When are you gonna realize that I want you to have everything in life that you want? So, of course I mean it."

I give him a small smile. "Thanks."

He winks, and his boots stomp on the floor of my cottage before the door closes behind him. I lean against the wall, needing something to hold me up. Maybe I should just say screw it all and tell the man I love him. But then again, I need him too much right now. Regardless of me wishing I could do this myself, I know I probably can't. Jude knows it, and I know it, even if I don't want to admit that to him yet. So I'll keep my feelings to myself a little longer.

❧

Downtown Willowbrook is quaint with the bank on the corner of the square. I park my yellow 1969 Datsun that my grandma gave me when I graduated high school in the angled parking spot in front of the bank. Then I check myself in the mirror one last time.

"You are a good investment," I tell myself over and over.

A few people are walking along the sidewalk as I step out of the car. One woman looks at me and turns to her friend to say something. Her friend glances over her shoulder at me as I step up onto the sidewalk. Whatever. Sometimes I wonder what it would've been like if I had gone to college after high school. I probably would've come back anyway. I'm all my parents have—all my mom has now.

I swallow past the grief that threatens to pour over me like a rogue wave and pull the door to the bank open.

Soft music plays, and the two tellers are huddled together in what appears to be a gossipy conversation. One looks my way, and they break apart.

"Sadie," she says, smiling. "What can I help you with?"

Cora went to high school with us. She was on my debate team. I really hope she can help me with this, but I fear it will be Mrs. Doyle I have to deal with. She's great, but I know for certain she's the queen bee of the Willowbrook gossip chain.

"How're Alvin and the boys?"

She nods. "They're good. Thank you for asking. I'm sorry to hear about your dad."

"Thank you...I wanted to talk to someone about a loan."

Her smile drops for a second, but she quickly plasters it back in place. "Oh." She looks past me, and my stomach drops. Mrs. Doyle it is. "You have to talk to Mrs. Doyle about it." From her expression, she has the same thoughts about the woman that I do. "Let me check with her first."

She rounds the desk and slips into an office behind me.

I smile politely at the other woman, who I'm not familiar with, but from her pitying expression, she knows my story. Seriously, this town.

"Sadie?" Cora pulls my attention from behind me, and I turn around. "She can see you now."

"Thank you so much."

As I pass, Cora touches my arm and squeezes it, giving me a soft smile. Cora is one of the good ones.

I peek my head into the office. "Mrs. Doyle?"

"Sadie Wilkins, come in." She waves me in. Her red hair is pulled back into a bun, and her glasses sit on the tip of her nose. "How are you?"

There it is. It's amazing how the cadence and sound of the words can change the meaning of a question so much.

"I'm good."

"And your mom?"

I nod my head from side to side.

"Understandable. Grief is hard and hits you in unexpected ways."

"Yes, I'm finding that to be true."

Just the other night, I'd been fine, doing research on my idea to regenerate the land. The fact that I didn't know how my dad would feel about it hit me, quickly spiraling into thoughts about how if I ever get married, he won't walk me down the aisle, and my kids will never know him. That I wasted all these years, and now he's gone.

"If you or your mom need anything, you'll let me know?"

"We will. Thank you, Mrs. Doyle."

She leans back in her chair, and I know she probably knows exactly what I want, why I'm here. "How can I help you? Cora said you were looking into a loan?"

"Yes."

She nods, but I hear her heavy sigh. She stands and rounds her desk, shutting the door. Not the best sign. "I'm gonna be truthful with you, Sadie. Your dad has been in here numerous times to get a loan, and each time I told him…" She sits down and takes off her glasses, clasping her hands on her desk. "The bank just won't approve it."

"But—"

"Sadie. I'm sorry."

"But I have ideas, plans." I open my bag and pull out the business plan I drew up and lay it on her desk.

She picks up her glasses and looks it over. That has to be good, right?

"I want to regenerate the land. Turn it into a chicken farm, pasture-raised."

47

I hate the smile she gives me. It's not one of "what a great idea, we'll give you whatever you want." "These are great, and I think you have a good idea, especially with the part of the land your dad couldn't plant on this year, but it comes down to how will you pay it back if this fails?"

"I'm good for it. You know I am."

She leans back, taking off her glasses and biting down on the end of one arm. "I wish I could approve a loan for you, but I can't."

"I—" I knew it was a long shot, but I had to try.

"Could you get someone to cosign for you?" she asks.

It's something I know my dad would have never considered, and I won't either. I'm not attaching other people to my family debt. Who would I ask, Bruce Noughton? Give me a break. I might as well trek up the hill to the Crawford family and be like, "You seem to have come into money, can you tell me how? Or better yet, can you loan me some?"

"No."

She looks at the office door behind me then leans forward over the desk. "I will say...if you were married, and your husband had land or some sort of collateral..."

"Married? Husband?" I frown.

"I don't think I need to spell this out for you." Mrs. Doyle grins as if she just gave me the winning lottery ticket.

I blink several times. "Jude?"

"He is a Noughton, and you know they bank here, so..."

How is this woman the manager of a bank? I want to put my hands over my ears and shake my head like a toddler. "We're just friends."

"Are you really?"

"Yes." I roll my eyes, collecting my papers and putting them back in my bag. "Thank you for taking the time to see me." I stand.

"I'm just making a suggestion, Sadie. You marry a Noughton, and your worries go away."

I'm struck with disbelief that she would suggest that. I can't even tell Jude that I love him. How can I ask him to marry me just so I can use his land for collateral? No way. I'll figure it out, find another way. Maybe the Crawford family isn't a bad idea.

"Thank you, Mrs. Doyle."

"Anytime, Sadie. Give me a call if you need anything."

I walk out of her office, waving to Cora and ignoring her sympathetic smile. Stepping out of the bank into the sun, I tip my head back, allowing the sun to heat my skin.

Back to step one.

I straighten and walk to my car, but a big body next to a truck draws me in first. He's showered and dressed in a fresh pair of jeans and T-shirt that draws tight along his biceps and chest. His hair isn't tucked under a cowboy hat and is still damp at the ends.

"Jude? What are you doing here?"

Chapter Six

JUDE

When I left Sadie at her cottage, I wasn't planning on cutting the day short after lunch, but Lottie's words rang through my head on my way back to the ranch. *She's going to lose it soon.* I knew the bank appointment wouldn't go how she wanted it to, so I decided to let Emmett handle the rest of the day on his own with the hopes he doesn't burn the place to the ground.

She steps out of the bank wearing that damn dress that's driving me fucking crazy. When she came out of her bedroom, I wanted to suggest she look through her mom's closet. The way it dips in the front, teasing her cleavage...I purposely hung my hands from her doorframe to keep them to myself, but even then, I couldn't stop myself from leaning into her small bathroom to smell her. I'm fucking pathetic. And I can't even think about her in that towel unless I want to sport a hard-on all goddamn day.

"Jude? What are you doing here?"

I push off my truck and step onto the sidewalk. "Hey."

"Hey. What's going on?"

"I'm taking you to lunch."

She glances at the town clock on the edge of the bank building. "It's after one."

"I haven't eaten. Have you?"

She hasn't. Lunch is the one meal she usually skips, which puts her on edge when she comes over for dinner if I'm running late preparing it.

She rolls her eyes, thinking I'm going to lecture her, but she's got a lot more to worry about than whether she ate lunch.

"Come on. I'll take you for tacos."

Her face lights up, her smile piercing my heart like the tip of a hot needle. "You're not going to tell me I told you so?"

"No, I'm going to take you to lunch." I take her hand and lead her to my truck.

"What about my car?"

"We'll come back and pick it up after."

I open up my truck door, and she steps up on the running boards, climbing in. The skirt of her dress slips and reveals her bare leg. I clench the door with my fist and shut it, getting a hold of myself as I round the front of the truck.

"Hi, Jude." Laurel, Gillian's best friend, side-eyes me as she grabs the handle of the door to the bank. She waves to Sadie. "Date night?"

"It's lunchtime, Laurel."

Her eyes run over my body, though not in an appraising way. She cocks an eyebrow and giggles to herself. "Well...don't do anything that earns you a spot on The Canary Post." Her laughter continues as she opens the bank door and disappears inside.

I climb into the driver's seat, and Sadie is looking at me. "What did Laurel say? Her new haircut looks cute."

I start the truck and place my hand on the back of Sadie's headrest, reversing out of the angled parking spot. "She says hi."

"I should've gotten out to say thanks. She sent over muffins to my mom yesterday."

I'm used to people like Laurel implying that Sadie and I are more than friends. The Willowbrook rumor mill is constantly speculating that we're sleeping together or, for some reason, hiding a relationship, which makes no sense. My brothers constantly razz me about why I haven't gone for Sadie, but I've always kept my feelings close to my chest. Since my mom died, Sadie's been the woman in my life, and just when I think I'm ready to tell her how I feel, I hesitate, fear-stricken that I'll fuck it all up and lose her all together. I'm not loveable like Ben or Emmett. I'm a grumpy asshole most of the time.

"I'm sure she knows you're thankful. I'm starving." I drive us to El Taco Cabana and park in the lot.

We both get out and meet on the sidewalk in front of my truck, walking to the door.

Ramon grabs two menus when he sees us come in. I'm not sure Willowbrook would have such great authentic Mexican food if Ramon Martinez hadn't opened a restaurant using his grandmother's recipes after he graduated from high school.

"Do you even need these?" Ramon asks, holding up the menus.

Sadie laughs and shakes her head. "Probably not."

He drops them back on the hostess stand. "I figured. How are you guys? Lunch, huh?"

He walks us to our usual booth in the front corner, so we can watch the people go by, but still have a little privacy.

Sadie slides in on the one side, and I slide in across from her. "Jude surprised me."

Ramon raises his eyebrows at me. "And you're wearing a dress, and Jude's all cleaned up. Did something change?"

Sadie grows quiet so I take the reins. "It's just lunch, Ramon."

Ramon nods, but I see his mind working. Sometimes I wonder what would happen if Sadie found some guy and dated him. What would the town think then? Although the thought of Sadie giving her sweet smiles to someone else causes my adrenaline to spike into rage mode.

"Enjoy, Sabrina will be out in a moment."

We both thank him, and he walks into the kitchen.

Sadie looks out the window.

"So, are you going to tell me what happened?" I ask.

Usually, Sadie isn't quiet like she was on the ride over here. Maybe it's because she has so much on her mind, or maybe because her dad passed, but before all this, she was always talking to me about something. I've always appreciated her ability to keep our conversations going since I keep a lot to myself.

"You were right. They won't give me the money. I didn't even get to show her the plan I put together."

"I wish I'd been wrong just this one time."

One side of her lips tips up.

"Do you want to show me the plans?"

"No." She glances toward the kitchen.

"Come on."

"You'll think it's stupid, and after Mrs. Doyle, I need a breather from shitty news."

Sabrina comes over and places two waters and some chips and salsa on the table. "Hey, you two. Lunch date?"

I groan, and Sadie kicks me under the table. Why is it such a big deal that we're out for lunch?

I eye her with a warning glare, but she ignores me and smiles at Sabrina. "How are you?"

"I should be asking you that. I'm sorry to hear about your dad." She gives Sadie a sympathetic look, then pulls out her pen and notepad.

"Thank you." Sadie doesn't bother looking at me, though

my eyes remain on her, still waiting for the fallout I'm sure is coming. At some point, she's going to break down when people keep talking to her about her dad. "I'll have my usual."

"Perfect." Sabrina writes it down and looks at me. "You too?"

"Yeah, thanks."

"It'll be right up." Sabrina leaves.

I watch her until she's back in the kitchen. The restaurant isn't busy today. There's only one other couple in the back on the other side, though I don't recognize them.

I turn my attention back to Sadie. "C'mon, show it to me."

"Can we drop it? You're supposed to be cheering me up."

"When did I promise that?" I ask, leaning forward. I might not have said it, but we both know that's why I showed up at the bank. "C'mon, I'm your best friend."

Her gaze strays to her bag next to her. If she were my brother, I'd snatch it before she could stop me.

"Let's just eat."

"Sadie, I'm here to listen and talk this out."

"I appreciate it, but I just want to wallow in some tacos."

"At least tell me what Mrs. Doyle said."

She blows out a breath and stares out the window again. "She said no. She said that my dad had been there multiple times, and we have nothing to give them if we can't repay the money. So, that's a dead end."

I take a sip of my water, thinking maybe I should've let the topic be, allowed her to process it all and come up with her next plan. "Once we harvest the soybeans, you'll get some money."

"Which won't be enough. I've looked through all the papers, and I think I might just have to sell." She sighs, and her shoulders sink.

My heart sinks because I don't have the money to give her.

If I did, I would, and although Ben does, I don't want him to step in. My ego and my pride dictate that Sadie is mine to protect. I need to figure this out for her. I'm honestly not sure she would accept Ben's money anyway.

"She said if I could find a cosigner, then maybe they'd approve the loan. But whoever I got would have to have collateral."

My head spins with the knowledge that my dad added my name to the ranch after I turned eighteen. Each of us Noughton boys owns a portion, but I've turned the ranch around. It's worth quite a lot now. "I'll cosign."

"No." She shakes her head, picking up her water glass and gulping down a good portion. "I'm not mixing anyone else up in this."

"It's the only way. Show me your plans. We can be business partners." I'll have to talk to my dad because I'm not sure how it works since there's more than just my name on the ranch, but I know between Sadie and me, we can get her farm going.

"I'm not complicating our relationship with business. Thank you, but no."

Sabrina comes over and places chicken tacos in front of Sadie and steak ones in front of me. "Here you go. Let me know if you need anything else. I'll be back to check on you in a bit."

"Looks great," Sadie says.

We thank Sabrina, and Sadie picks up a taco, taking a bite and moaning as she chews. I shift in my seat. Gets me every damn time.

"Now I'm happy," she says after she swallows.

I bite into my steak taco, and when I'm done chewing, I approach the subject one more time. "If you don't want to show me your business plan, will you at least tell me what you're thinking?"

56

Her gaze falls to her plate. "You're going to say it's stupid."

"No, I won't. Come on."

"I haven't told anyone. Not even Lottie."

I try not to be offended that she says it as if Lottie is close to me on Sadie's friend meter.

We continue eating for a few more bites, and I wait because I'm fairly sure she's going to break and tell me.

I'm on my second taco when she finally says, "Chickens."

"Chickens?"

She wipes her mouth with her napkin and clasps her hands in her lap. "I want to breed pasture-raised chickens. Regenerate the land and use it for chickens."

That was not on my radar. I assumed maybe she'd want to expand her garden, grow something different than soybeans, but chickens...we have a few on Plain Daisy Ranch, but mostly only for Jensen, who wants them for their eggs. The rest go to The Harvest Depot to sell.

"Interesting idea."

She points at me. "See, I knew you'd shoot it down."

I drop my third taco and shake my head. "I'm not shooting it down. I just wasn't prepared for you to say that."

"I know it will take some time, and I'd have to wait until early spring to start, but I could use the winter to prepare. I've been watching a lot of videos, and I'm thinking about going to see this guy who started his own chicken farm five years ago."

Red flags wave in my head. Guy?

"Who's this guy?" I frown.

"Just someone I've been conversing with online. He has these how-to videos online, and I started messaging him. He knows so much about it."

My hand clenches the taco, and it falls apart.

"Did your tortilla get soggy?" She looks at my now crumpled up steak and tortilla on my plate.

"Yeah," I lie. I hate that she's talking to some guy and

might go see him. Everything inside me says to put a stop to it, so I say something I'm not sure I can even pull off. "Chickens are a great idea. I'll help you get started."

"Well, not yet. I still have the issue with the mortgage. The farm might not even be in my family next year." I can hear the pain in her voice at the thought of that.

"I'm sure we'll figure it out." I dip a chip into the salsa.

She stares at me long and hard until my gaze meets hers. "Don't try to be the savior here. I'm not taking anyone else down with me."

I chew and swallow, chuckling to myself. "You know as well as I do, it's either both of us or neither of us."

We finish our meals, then I drop her off at her car before driving back to the ranch. Now I have to convince another person to go along with my plan, and I'm pretty sure I'm going to need to do a good sales job to get him to say yes.

Chapter Seven

JUDE

My dad is out by Bessie when I get back to the ranch. She's our Guernsey cow, and although we no longer milk her, she's like our ranch mascot. A lot of us spend some time with her every day, and I can't deny that I've told her a lot of my problems over the years.

"Hey, Dad," I say, and he pushes himself off the fence.

"Heard you took the afternoon off. Just so we're clear, when I said to take your brother under your wing, I didn't mean abandon him."

"All he had to do—"

"I'm not getting into this his-word-against-yours bullshit. If you want to enjoy more afternoons off, train your brother properly. End of discussion."

I stuff my hands in my pockets, not about to argue with my dad. I'm sure Emmett went to Dad and cried that I just left him, but he's only four years younger than me, and he's worked the ranch most of his life. I shouldn't have to detail to him what needs to be done. But I set aside my irritation. I have a bigger agenda on my mind.

"How's Sadie?" Dad asks, patting Bessie's side before walking back to the house.

"She's okay. Took her to lunch."

"I figured." My dad has never said one word to me about whether Sadie and I are more than just friends, like everyone else. "Rhea said she's been asking a lot of questions, and Rhea doesn't have the answers. She feels a lot of guilt, wishes she'd had Monty talk to Sadie."

"He should've. I mean, how could he do this and never have told her?"

I'm pissed at Mr. Wilkins on Sadie's behalf. No one knows if it would have been different had he been upfront with her, but at least she could be grieving instead of trying to tread water in a damn hurricane.

"Monty was old-school. He was raised to believe you keep your problems away from your kids. If Sadie had been a boy, I'm not sure it would've been different. It was just his way. You don't burden the ones you love with your problems."

I think back to when I was younger, and our ranch was on the brink. If it happened now, would my dad have told Ben, Emmett, or me? I'd like to say yes, but I guess it's time to stop blaming Monty and move forward toward a solution.

"I want to talk to you about something."

"No." He opens the screen door at the front of our family home.

Not much has changed over the years. My dad refuses to renovate. There's still wood paneling on the walls of our family room. Although there's a flat-screen television now, the couches are still the original brown-and-orange plaid. It's how Mom decorated our home. A family picture taken only a few months before she died hangs above the fireplace. Sometimes I worry that my dad got stuck after she died and refuses to remove anything related to her. But then he brings women home, so I guess I really don't understand him. Her death affected us all in different ways, that I do know.

I follow him to the kitchen. "You don't even know what I'm going to ask."

He opens the fridge and takes out Jensen's chicken salad, which everyone loves. "You're going to ask me if you can co-sign a loan for Sadie."

I slide up on the counter as he grabs a loaf of bread out of our bread box and a knife out of the drawer. "How did you know that?"

"She went to the bank today. Word travels."

"Damn Mrs. Doyle. How unethical is that?"

He busies himself making a sandwich. "It's Willowbrook."

I sigh. "Why's the answer no?"

The back door swings open, and Emmett stops just inside the door, pointing at me. "You're an asshole. You left me with a bunch of kindergarteners."

I chuckle.

He scowls at me. "Seriously, I had to give them a tour of the farm."

"That is the only reason kindergarteners would be at the ranch," I say.

"Screw you. You're lucky their teacher was hot."

"If you'd paid more attention to the class rather than the teacher, that one kid wouldn't have snuck under the fencing and slipped on a pile of shit." My dad stops slicing the tomato to give Emmett the stern eye we're so used to being on the receiving end of.

"Did you see her? No joke, Jude, she would've had you sayin' Sadie who?" Emmett grabs the juice pitcher out of the fridge.

I pretend to look at my watch. "Did I miss a few hours, and it's already five o'clock? Why are you in here?"

He ignores me and grabs a glass from the cupboard next to

me, jabbing me in the rib. I kick my leg out to the side, hitting him square in the thigh.

"All right, enough. Emmett, tours are a good way to make sure the kids around here respect the land and that some will want to be ranchers themselves. We've done them for years, and that's not going to change. Get used to it."

"If the teachers all look like Miss Anderson, I'm in." He sits at the table, pouring his juice.

"Yeah, can you take that to go?" I say to him.

Emmett leans back in his chair, stretching out his legs and crossing his ankles with a shit-eating grin. "Not on your life. What are we talking about?" He looks between Dad and me.

"None of your business."

"He's part of the decision too," my dad says.

"No, he's not." My jaw hardens.

Emmett raises his hand, inching it up and down over and over. "Oh. Oh. Can I guess?"

"No," my dad and I say in unison.

"Jude riding in on his white horse?"

"Fuck off." I scowl at him.

He taps his finger to his lips. "You might have to go to Hickory to that costume store to find a knight's costume. But if they don't have one, and you want to go to Lincoln, I'm up for a road trip."

I narrow my eyes at him. "Sadie doesn't need saving. She'll save herself."

"With your safety net," Emmett says.

Disregarding him, I concentrate on my dad. He carries his plate to the table, kicking the bottom of Emmett's boots. Emmett sits up straight and sips his juice.

"We can't risk our farm to save theirs." Dad takes a bite of his sandwich.

Emmett looks at me while our dad chews and swallows, concentrating on his next bite.

"You know I can get that ranch up and going. Look what I did here." I jump off the counter, taking the seat between them. "Monty didn't have the equipment nor the connections we do. Come on, Dad. She needs us."

Surprisingly, Emmett says nothing.

Dad puts his sandwich down and sighs. "I'd love to, but it's too risky, and…" He sighs again. "She's not family."

"What?" My mouth opens and closes like a gaping fish.

"Seriously, Dad?" Emmett's forehead wrinkles. "Rhea was mom's best friend. Sadie is Jude's. She's family."

Dad leans back in his chair, crosses his arms, and sets his gaze on me. "She's *like* family, but she's not family. She could go down to The Hidden Cave and fall head over heels for some guy, marry him, and then he takes over the ranch. What are you gonna do then?"

The tacos in my stomach sour at the image he's placed in my head. "Sadie wouldn't."

"She's thirty-three, Jude. She's never been shy about wanting a husband and a family one day." My dad's gaze doesn't leave mine.

I glance at Emmett, whose eyebrows raise. He tilts his head, agreeing with Dad it seems. "She is getting older."

"I thought you were on my side."

Emmett holds up his hands. "I see both sides. Sadie is family, and I want to help, but I see what Dad's saying too."

"Sadie isn't going to marry someone else." I rock back on my chair, teetering on the back two legs.

"Else?" Emmett raises an eyebrow.

I flip him off. "Someone. She's not going to marry anyone while she's trying to get that farm going."

"You know how long it's going to take her to pay off the loan she needs to pay the mortgage plus start something new? Did she even tell you what her plans are? Because soybeans aren't going to do it for her. I tried to tell Monty." Dad takes the last bite of his sandwich and the room quiets.

The two of them are waiting for me to tell them, but I find I'm nervous. The longer they stare at me, waiting, the more I dread it.

"She wants to raise free-range chickens."

Dad nods and stands, taking his plate to the sink.

"That's a shit-ton of work," Emmett whispers as if Dad can't hear him.

"And here I thought this was a workday." Ben stands outside the screen door, his face pressed to the screen with his hands on either side of his face to peer inside. "What? I'm not part of the family meetings now?"

Ben walks in and takes the seat next to Emmett, stealing his cup of juice.

"Sadie wants to raise chickens. Free range." Emmett stares at my dad's back.

I give Sadie props—it's something I've been wanting to look into for the beef we produce, but I haven't had the time. I brought it up once to my dad, but his mantra is why change something that's working.

"That's awesome. It's gotta be more lucrative than soybeans, right?" With Ben being gone playing professional football since he was eighteen, he doesn't know much these days about ranch life. "Must cost some money to overhaul the farm though..."

Ben eyes me with an expression that says he's the solution. I want to haul him over the table and watch my fist collide with his smug face. I shake my head.

"We already decided Jude rides the white horse and we're going to Lincoln to buy a knight costume." Emmett smiles widely and sarcastically at me.

I flip him off again. He laughs.

"Is there a wedding ring in that costume too?" Ben asks, laughing along with Emmett.

"That's the only way Dad will let Jude cosign a loan for Sadie."

Fucking Emmett can't keep his mouth shut.

"I'll give you the loan for a better interest rate than the bank," Ben says, still wanting to be the hero.

"I wish things were different," Dad says, not sitting down which means he's done talking about this. "But as much as I love the Wilkinses, as much as I want to save their land, and as much as I view them as family, they aren't. There are too many variables, and I can't risk your future, your brothers, your aunts and uncles and cousins. I would never ask anyone to do that for us. I'm sorry, Jude."

Dad pats me on the shoulder, and I know it pains him. I know he wants all those things he said, and I hate that a small part of me agrees with him.

"Which is why Bank Ben is open. No marriage contingencies." Ben holds his arms open, waving his hands to welcome me into a hug.

"Fuck off." I stand and push the chair into the table, wood banging against wood.

I storm out of my dad's house, the screen door hitting the frame with a bang.

"So, when are we leaving for Lincoln?" Emmett shouts, and I hear Ben laugh.

I'm not a white knight kind of guy, but I also don't like being told no. So I head to my house to think over my options of how to get Sadie what she needs. Damn it if only one solution comes to my mind. A solution I'm not sure I can give her.

Chapter Eight

SADIE

"Hi, Mom."

She's sitting in her chair, watching the latest popular game show. She's always been a game show addict.

"Hi, Sadie," she says and reaches for the remote, but I shoo her to stop.

I sit on the couch next to her recliner. The recliner that sits next to my dad's now-empty one, both worn in from years of sitting here and watching game shows. They used to play this game as if they could select a team and compete against one another. Now it's just Mom playing by herself, and that makes my chest ache.

"Want me to be Team Kevin?" I ask, ready to spend some time with her before I head over to Jude's. I'm not sure I'll be able to concentrate on the crime show we've been bingeing, but I would love to get out of my head if only for a few hours.

"No, sweetie, don't worry about me." She takes me in. "You look lovely this evening."

She smiles, and I grab her hand. "I'm going to get us out of this."

Her gaze runs over the room and the scattered pictures of

the three of us throughout the years. "I think we should sell. Just let it go. I'll find an apartment, and you start that life you should've been living after high school." Her small frail hand squeezes mine with as much strength as she can muster.

I shake my head. "No. I'm going to figure it out."

She gives me an expression as if to tell me to listen to her. "This land is important, but I'm convinced the stress of trying to make the payments caused your dad his heart attack. I don't want you to have a life like he did, we did. You don't need to be stressed every season about crop growth and whether the weather will cooperate and what the price of goods and fuel is. This is your chance to go live your own life, and I want you to take it."

I shake my head, and she sighs. Her hair is pulled back, the few gray strands blending into her blonde hair that matches my own. She doesn't look nearly as old as I think she feels some days.

"I have an idea. I just have to find the money to execute it and pay the mortgage."

She tilts her head, questioning how that might even be possible.

"I will find it, Mom." My voice is filled with determination.

"You don't have to save this place. Your dad never wanted to burden you. He always blamed himself for you not getting out of Willowbrook like you wanted." Her words are shaky, as if she might break down in tears. "I told him that's my burden to bear."

"No, Mom, I'm happy here. I'm not sure what I would've done had I left anyway."

"You're happily stuck in a town with no marriage prospects? If you'd left at eighteen, you'd be successful and probably married by now. Your dad would've been a grandpa, and now..." Tears slip down her cheeks.

"Mom. No. We can't rewind time, and I'm happy to be in Willowbrook. I've made a life here."

I'm not going to tell her how lost I felt after I finished community college and the two years of driving back and forth to Lincoln to get my bachelor's degree in graphic design were done. Because I had to take my mom to all her doctor's appointments, I couldn't get a full-time job, so I'd take on freelance graphic design jobs and do designs for my dad that he never really used. It was difficult at first, but I made my peace and settled in. I like my life now.

"But your life could be more. Go move to a big city, use that degree of yours, and have some new experiences. Meet the man of your dreams."

My mom has to know my feelings for Jude. Doesn't the entire town know I want Jude Noughton to the point I can't imagine myself with anyone else?

"I'm staying here and going to turn the land into a chicken farm." My tone is firm.

She removes her hand from mine and raises it to my cheek, cradling it in her palm as if I'm five again. "That's a lot of work, sweetie."

"I know, but I've done a lot of research. It doesn't take nearly as much as you'd think."

She shakes her head, and her matching green eyes meet mine. "I'd like you to take this time for yourself. I'm fine to go live in an apartment or an assisted living facility."

"You do not need to be in an assisted living facility. You'll live here, and after I'm done with the ranch, I'm going to fix up this house so you don't trip and fall."

Her thin lips tip, and all her love for me pours into her expression. "You're the best daughter a mom could ask for. Your dad too. He'd say all the time how proud he was of you."

Proud but never trusted me. My chest aches.

"I got lucky too."

Her smile deepens. "Go enjoy being young."

I laugh and cover her hand on my cheek with my own. "Call me if you need me?"

"I'll be fine. *Price is Right* is next. You know how I love bidding."

"All right. Love you."

"Love you."

I stand and grab my purse from the end of the couch, walking to the door.

"Please think about what I said, Sadie."

I turn back to her, and my shoulders fall. "I will."

I figure that's better than fighting about it more. I love that she wants me to go out and explore the world, but my life is here now, on my family farm, with friendships that have only deepened throughout the years. So I'll let her believe I'm thinking about leaving, but it's not even a consideration.

I drive under the iron arch that reads Plain Daisy Ranch and follow the road past the Noughton family home in the direction of the other homes that surround the lake. I'm not sure why Bruce never built a new house on the water, although I'm sure it has something to do with his late wife and the home they built together.

I pass Ben and Emmett's drives and turn onto Jude's. I still find it crazy that he built his own house. I always wondered why a man who has never talked about getting married would build a four-bedroom home with a big kitchen for entertaining.

The lights are on in the family room and kitchen, and his favorite country music plays while he cooks. I knock on the screen door, and he peeks over his shoulder.

"Hey," he says with one of his heart-wrenching smiles.

It's only heart-wrenching because I wish he was giving me that smile when I was waking up in his bed.

I walk into the kitchen, and the smell of garlic fills my

nostrils, making my stomach growl. And I even ate lunch today.

He's at the kitchen sink, his back to me, and I admire the way his black T-shirt stretches across his shoulders and narrows at his waist. He's changed out of his jeans and into joggers, and god help me, he's barefoot. The kicker is, he's completely blind to the fact that I'm drooling behind him.

"Wine is in the fridge if you want some," he calls, grabbing the colander of green beans and putting them next to the cutting board on his island.

"Oh, you didn't have to." I slip off my sandals at the door and drop my purse on a kitchen chair.

"We're going to celebrate tonight." He doesn't look up, cutting off each green bean stem and placing them in another bowl.

"Celebrate?" I open his fridge and grab the bottle of white wine. My favorite brand. What in the world is going on?

"Yeah, mind grabbing me a beer?"

Before the door closes, I grab him a bottle of beer, then go over to the drawer where he keeps both openers. "What are we celebrating exactly?"

Still not looking up, he says, "Later. Let's eat first."

He takes the bowls to the stove, pours olive oil into a pan, and dumps in the green beans.

As I open the bottle of wine, I see another pot on the stove. "What are we having?"

"Garlic ranch mashed potatoes and salmon along with those biscuits you ate five of last time." He grins at me. I hand him his beer while he moves the green beans around the oiled pan. "Thanks."

Grabbing a stool from his island, I sit and watch him work, knowing I should be asking what I can help with, but I'd really rather sit here and admire him.

Jeez, I need a hobby.

"Full disclosure, it was the day before my period."

"I'm not judging, just saying why I made them."

I sip my wine. "Which raises the question...why are you making all my favorite foods?"

He chuckles and wipes his hands on a dish towel before throwing it over his shoulder. "Can't I do something nice for you?"

Jude does a lot of nice things for me, but I'm not sure he's ever made an entire meal of all my favorite foods. He hates green beans, and usually, it's an argument about what vegetables we're going to eat. He loves asparagus, and I'm a green bean lover, especially when they're cooked on the stove with oil and seasonings only he can perfect.

"You mentioned celebrating, but you're in joggers with no socks."

He looks down at himself as though he doesn't remember what he changed into after his shower. "I should've dressed up."

My head tilts. "Why?"

He picks up a hot pad and removes the salmon from the oven, placing it on the stove. "We're getting there."

"When?"

He grabs two plates and shakes his head, laughing to himself.

Knowing he's not going to tell me until he's good and ready, I enjoy my wine. "Whatever." I refill my wine glass. The crisp cool sweetness is too good not to have another serving. "So...my mom told me to let the farm go."

He stops mashing the potatoes for a second, but then his forearm flexes as he hammers the masher up and down again. "She did?"

"She said it was time for me to leave Willowbrook."

Again, he stops mashing for the briefest of seconds, but he doesn't look at me. "What did you say?"

"I told her no. My life is here. I told her about my idea for the chicken farm. She liked it."

He pulls the masher from the potatoes, pounding it against the edge of the metal pot, and the remaining potatoes fall back into the pot. "Oh."

I know he'd be upset if I left Willowbrook. I would be upset if he did.

"She said she'd move into assisted living. Leave the land and house to just go up for auction. Why would I do that?"

He places the masher in the sink and wipes his hands on the towel, leaning against the counter, his eyes on me. "It makes sense. Maybe you should do it."

"What?"

He breaks the distance, picking up his beer and gulping a few mouthfuls before coming to the other side of the island. "You should've gotten out of here a long time ago."

My heart cracks. Jude wants me to leave? If he were leaving, I'd throw myself on his hood, telling him I was going with him. But Jude doesn't have that luxury because his obligation is to the farm. Well, mine is too. My mom is dependent on me, just as so many are dependent on Jude for the ranch to be successful.

"I don't want to."

"Why not?" He finishes his beer.

I haven't seen him finish one so fast since Ben's welcome home party. I sip my own wine. "Why am I not going to leave?"

"Why do you want to stay here, Sadie?" His hands are on the edge of the counter, his arms flexed as he leans toward me, his dark coffee-stained eyes drilling into mine.

"This is my home."

"And it always will be. You can leave and come home whenever you want."

"Why are you asking me this?" Anger bubbles inside me.

Why is he always so willing to cast me out to sea when I'm desperate to have him reel me in?

"I just want to know where your head is." He goes to the fridge and grabs another beer.

What is going on with him tonight?

"It's here. In Willowbrook. Along with my heart. I want to turn my family's land into a chicken farm. That's my dream now...well, one of them anyway." I slide off the stool, rounding the island to face him. "Now, what are we celebrating?"

He places his beer bottle on the counter. "So, you want to stay in Willowbrook? You're sure?"

"Jude! What the hell?"

He bites his bottom lip and stares at the floor, then he looks at me. "Answer the question," he says so softly I barely hear him.

His chocolate eyes look into my green ones, and I see such a mix of emotions in his that I can't make sense of them. "Yes. I'm not going anywhere."

He slides his hand into his pocket.

"What is going on with you tonight?" I ask.

He lifts his hand toward the counter and opens his palm before pulling his hand away. "Marry me, Sadie."

I stare at the silver band with a beautiful round diamond sparkling in the center. My heart gallops, and my gaze rises to his.

Where did I miss the fork in the road this time?

Chapter Nine

SADIE

His eyes aren't pouring over with love. His hands aren't shaking from nerves. His smile isn't full and wide. My heart slows to a trot before stalling completely because Jude's not asking me to marry him because he loves me.

I've waited and wished for this day, but not like this. Not for the reason he's asking.

I close my eyes, place my finger in the middle of the ring, and push it back to him. "No."

Grabbing my wine, I walk out of the house and step out on the porch. I hear him turn off the burners, his beer sliding off the counter, and the porch screen door opens behind me.

"Why?"

I stare at the water and the two ducks that have been present all season, swimming side by side. I hug the pillar of the porch and drink my wine. "I'm not trapping you in some sham of a marriage."

"You're not trapping me if I'm doing the asking."

He doesn't face the lake, instead resting his backside on the railing and staring at me. His arms are crossed, and he has a beer in his hand.

"Why would you ask me?"

"Honestly?"

"Yes."

"I asked my dad if I could cosign for you, and he said no."

My stomach sinks. I never expected Jude to put his family farm on the line to save my family's dinky one. But the fact that Bruce said no puts a line in the sand that does hurt a little if I'm honest. He's always made me feel like family, but it's a reminder that I'm not. "Got it."

He slides down the railing, closer to me. "Of course, he wants to help any way he can, but he can't put my family's farm in jeopardy not knowing if..."

I turn to look at him. "What?"

His expression says he doesn't want me to make him say it. "What, Jude?"

"He's worried about what would happen if I cosigned, then you found someone you wanted to be with..." He swallows hard. "To marry."

First my mom and now Bruce. Does the older generation really not know that I'm madly in love with Jude?

"So if we just get married, that eliminates the possibility of that. And as my wife, it solves the problem of me not being able to cosign."

I down the rest of my wine. "Just get married?"

He shrugs. "Yeah, we're best friends. It'd be easy. You can move in here, and we'll pretend for everyone's sake. Tell them we've been seeing each other in secret for a long time and decided to come out."

I turn away from the lake and place my wine glass on the railing. "No one is going to believe that."

"We just have to be convincing."

"You mean we'll just be engaged, right? Not actually get married?"

He shakes his head, the corner of his lips tipping down.

"No, we'd have to get married. We can elope or have a town wedding. It's up to you. The sooner we get it done, the better chance of you getting the loan processed."

I strip my gaze from him. "You make it sound so easy." I walk off the porch and back into his house.

He follows me. "It is easy."

"No. It's not. It's complicated. Very complicated. What if we get married, I get the loan, and I fail?"

He chuckles. "You won't."

I throw my hands in the air. "You don't know that, Jude." I try to calm myself. "I can't. I appreciate it, I really do. You're trying to help me, and I appreciate it, but I'll get myself out of this."

He glowers across the room at me. "You're being stubborn." He moves to the stove and plates the two dishes.

"Me not agreeing to marry you just to get you to cosign a big loan is being stubborn?"

He drops the spatula on the stove and whips around, raising his voice. "It's the only solution you have, Sadie. Don't you see that? You either marry me or lose the farm. There is no other choice for you. Unless you want to take money from Ben."

His sour tone draws me back. "I would never. And don't yell at me."

"Well, I'm sorry if I'm offended that you don't want to marry me."

My head rears back, and I look around as if someone is going to pop up with a camera and say this is a prank. "You're offended?"

"You won't let me help you."

"Marriage is no small thing, Jude!"

He stares long and hard at me. "You think I don't know that? You're the only person I'd even entertain this idea for. And you go and shoot me down."

A laugh slips out. Then I continue to laugh, unable to stop myself.

"Why are you laughing?" Jude turns his back to me, continuing to serve up the plates.

"We're arguing like a real couple about you fake-proposing to me."

He brings the plates to the island counter and sets them down, then opens the drawer and pulls out two forks. "I'm just trying to help."

I wrap my arms around his neck. He draws me in with his arms around my waist. God, it feels so good. Too good.

"Please, Sadie. Marry me so I can help you. We're going to make that farm the most successful chicken farm in the state. But you have to marry me to make that happen."

I close my eyes, burying my head in his neck. There's another reason I don't want to do this besides putting his own farm in jeopardy. What if the line blurs, and I fall even harder for Jude? Or if at some point, the lie comes out...I'm not sure I can handle the fallout.

"Jude..."

He draws back, taking my left hand. Sliding the ring off the counter, he holds it over the tip of my left ring finger. "What do you say?"

I blow out a breath, unsure of what to do. I'm not sure if it's because he's so close, the smell of the soap and shampoo he uses, the fact that he was offended by me saying no, or the meal he prepared for me. I have no rational reason to accept his proposal, but I still find myself saying, "Yes."

The metal slides onto my finger, and we both stare at it. It's a symbol of love, but that has nothing to do with the reason it's on my finger. My heart pinches at that, but it does look beautiful on my hand.

"Thank you. I can never thank you enough."

He shakes his head. "You don't have to thank me, especially since I had to convince you."

I laugh, secretly loving that I'm going to marry Jude Naughton, who's had my heart for decades.

"Now let's talk logistics," he says.

And that right there is what I have to remember every time butterflies fill my stomach—this ring came with an agenda.

We sit at the island, and Jude tells me the plan he's come up with for us to pull this off.

❧

THE NEXT MORNING, I WALK INTO THE HARVEST Depot before it's open for the day. Lottie is in the back, labeling the stock that Jensen brought over from the kitchen at The Getaway Lodge. He makes all the salads they sell and does quick sandwiches for people to buy for lunch.

"Hey," I say, unsure how to start this conversation.

Jude and I agreed that telling Lottie the truth so she could help us pull this off was priority one. She's too close to both of us, and Jude said he knew she'd be the first one to be skeptical. We need her to help us sell this.

She looks up from what she's doing. "Whoa, this is an early morning for you." Her blonde hair is pulled into a high bun, and she's wearing the apron with the logo for The Harvest Depot she had me create last year.

"Are you alone?"

Her head draws back. "What's going on? You've never come to see me before the store opens."

"Are you?"

She nods. "Jensen just left. What's up?"

She stops what she's doing and sits on a stool, patting the one across from her.

I slide onto it, tucking my left hand under my leg. "I need

to talk to you. You can't tell anyone what I'm about to tell you."

"Oh my god," she says. "Did you go over to Jude's in a whipped cream bikini and he turned you down? I'm gonna kill the bastard. Blood or not, he's dead to me."

"Lottie, why would you think I'd do that?"

"Well, you look so upset, and I figured you finally told him. If he'd have licked the whipped cream off your nipples, you wouldn't look sad."

I can't help but laugh at Lottie's thoughts that go haywire every once in a while. "First of all, that's not how I would go about telling Jude."

"It's hard for any guy to say no to that, though." She smiles at me like I know she's right.

I figure I need to get this over with quickly, especially since I'm not sure who could come in here at any time. So I raise my left hand in the air.

She grabs my hand, tugging me toward her, and I fall forward, almost face-planting between her legs. "Lottie!"

"Who?" she demands.

I wish I weren't smiling so much when I look at it or think about it. This is a marriage of convenience, nothing more. "Jude."

Her jaw slowly lowers, farther and farther. "Jude?"

I giggle. "Yep."

"So, you went over there and told him and what? He just had this ring waiting to propose to you? This is like a movie." She brings the ring closer to her eye as if she's a licensed diamond grader. "And it's so nice. Who would've thought Jude had taste like this? Not me."

My lips tip further, knowing he didn't have anyone help him since it's a secret.

She drops my hand, stands, and throws herself on me, leaning us right and left. "I'm so happy for you. It's everything you ever wanted."

80

I hate to be the pin to her balloon. "Not exactly."

She pulls back, her hands on my shoulders and eyes on mine. "What are you talking about?"

"I need a cosigner for the loan, and Bruce won't allow Jude to sign it unless we're married."

Her nose crinkles. "What? My uncle demanded that you marry Jude? Since when did our family turn psychotic? Oh god, am I next? They're going to auction me off...jeez. What if someone like Brooks wins?" She sticks her finger in her throat as if she's seven.

"It's not like that. Bruce doesn't know. Well..." I look at the clock, knowing Jude was going to tell him this morning. "He might know now."

"You have my mind everywhere. Tell me everything."

"Jude asked me to marry him last night, but only so he can cosign and get me the loan. It's not for love or because he really wants to. But I need you to keep that secret for us."

"You're going to marry him to save your farm?"

"It's my only choice."

She nods, and I wait for her thoughts. Rarely does Lottie not have an opinion. But she doesn't speak for a long time, and I worry she disagrees. "Well, whatever it takes. But are you going to be okay?"

I frown. "What do you mean?"

"I'm assuming you're going to play house with him."

"I have to."

"And Mommy and Daddy sleep in the same bed, right?"

I look down at my stomach. "I'm not pregnant."

"You know what I'm saying. I just don't want you to get hurt in the end."

Her lack of enthusiasm and the disappearance of her smile say what she really thinks of the plan, and I can't say I blame her. I've had second thoughts about a hundred times since last night.

"As long as I save the family farm, I'll be fine. That's what's most important."

She nods a few times as if trying to convince herself. "Well, if he hurts you, I'm going to sneak into his place in the middle of the night and wake him with a quick fist to his junk."

"I can handle myself, but we're good? You can keep the secret?"

"Of course." She pretends to zip her lips and throw out the key just like the first time I ever admitted my feelings for Jude to her.

"Lottie!" a male voice calls from the front of the store.

"Get out!" she shouts back and squeezes my hand. "I won't say a word, but be prepared, okay?"

"For what?"

"For the firing squad. If you're going to marry the most sought-after bachelor in Willowbrook, there are going to be some women who aren't very happy about it. But I've got your back." She winks and walks out of the back room.

"We're not open," she says to whoever is there.

I stand and steady myself for a moment. That's something I never thought about, how I'm not the only one who wants Jude Noughton. The last thing I want to be is the talk of this town or have people speculate that our marriage is a sham.

I follow Lottie out of the back room and find Brooks leaning along the door frame of the front door in his sheriff's uniform.

"Sadie, this is usually Lottie's and my time together." He smirks and eyes Lottie at the coffee station.

"I've been telling him for weeks that he's not welcome, but he shows up like a stray dog looking for his next meal." I quirk an eyebrow, and Lottie glares at me. "Don't think dirty thoughts, Sadie." She rounds the counter and thrusts the coffee at Brooks.

He grabs it before it spills, and he chuckles. "Thanks, and

I'm open to a hot meal anytime you wanna offer." His gaze falls between her thighs.

She pushes his shoulder. "Gross. Go!"

He chuckles, and she slams the door behind him, flipping the lock.

"Huh," I say.

She turns and looks at me. "What?"

"Nothing. Just nice of you to make him a coffee every morning."

"Don't you have to see a preacher about a wedding?"

I laugh, and she does too. At least I'll have Lottie to be my sounding board when all this goes terribly wrong.

Chapter Ten

JUDE

I'm probably picking the worst time to tell my dad, but I'm not interested in him calling me out in the kitchen of his house or, hell, calling a family meeting. We just got back from herding the cattle. I should at least ease into it, but that's not my style.

I put Titan back in his stall and shut the door. "I'm marrying Sadie."

Dad doesn't say anything, running a brush over Legend's mane.

"Did you hear me?"

"I heard you," he mumbles, continuing to groom his horse.

I was prepared for him to question me, tell me not to act like an idiot, and defy him. But we both know if he'd found himself in my position, he'd have done the same thing.

"I asked her last night. We're going to elope."

He puts down the brush, keeping his back to me. "Elope?"

"Yeah. I've been seeing her for months, and I was going to propose before Monty died." I hate lying to my dad. He's always had an open door for us when we sought out advice.

But I have no choice if we're going to sell this whole proposal thing. He's put me in this position, and I know that helping Sadie is the right thing to do.

"You have?" He turns around, shuts the stall door on Legend, and sits on the stool outside, resting his forearms on his legs. "Why were you keeping it a secret?"

That's a good question and not one I prepared myself for. Shit.

"You know this town."

"I do."

"We wanted to make sure it was going to work for us before anyone knew."

"And does it? Work?" His eyes pierce into mine. He's probably thinking he can sniff out my lie.

"Yeah."

"Not because I denied you cosigning unless you were married?"

I stuff my hands into my pockets and rock back on my boots. "Not at all."

He nods and looks outside the barn. It's a sunny fall day, and the weather is turning slightly cooler. "It's a no to the elopement then."

I stiffen. "What?"

He stands. "If you're going to marry Sadie Wilkins after all these years, you're not going to sneak off. You marry her at The Knotted Barn. I'm sure Romy can slide you in."

"We don't want a whole big thing. Just the two of us."

Lies. All lies. I'm pretty sure if I was marrying Sadie for real, she'd want a big wedding. Maybe not a huge one, but how many times when we were little did she make Emmett her groom because Ben and I refused? She'd pick wildflowers from the field and act as if they were her bridal bouquet.

"Are you going away to elope?" He stops at the edge of the

horse barn and stares at our cornfield. The one I have to plow soon for the maze we have every October.

"We were going to the courthouse."

He chuckles but stops before I question why he finds that humorous. "Son, let me give you some advice. There are a lot of women out there who would be okay with the courthouse. Others who want the destination wedding. But Sadie isn't one of them. Have you forgotten how she wore that flower girl dress for a month after she was in that wedding? If you love her, you give her what she wants. Don't half-ass this by going to the courthouse."

Does he really not see through everything I just threw at him? That getting married is a formality to secure the loan?

"Also, do you understand that marrying her means you're putting your stake in our land in jeopardy? There's no coming back and asking for another piece."

I gulp. I've thought about it, and it's a risk, but I'll bet on Sadie every damn time. And if something goes south, I'll figure it out. "I do."

He slaps me on the shoulder, and our eyes lock. "Congratulations, son. You're lucky you found someone as great as Sadie to spend your life with. Let me know what you need me to do."

He walks away before I can say anything, but he heads in the direction of the daisy hill cemetery. I wonder if it's to tell my mom that I've finally gotten my head out of my ass, and I'm marrying Sadie Wilkins.

"What to go for a ride?"

I turn to find Sadie at the opening of the other end of the barn. She's got her horse, Brownie, by the reins.

"I just put Titan in, but I'm sure he'd love to spend time with Brownie."

She laughs. Titan and Brownie have found a friendship

throughout the years due to the number of rides we've taken together.

I go to the stall and bring Titan back out. Saddling him up, we both hop on the horses and ride out toward the trail worn from years of riding around our land.

"I wanted to thank you," she says.

I really wish she would stop thanking me.

"It's a big deal, Jude, and I promise you won't lose your land."

"I'm not worried."

She moves ahead of me on the trail because we can't both fit through the opening between the trees, and I admire the nape of her neck. Her hair is braided today, and for a second, my memory flickers back to when we were younger, and she'd always be playing with the end of her braid. She's got jeans on and a short-sleeve shirt that's tight enough to show off her body but not be revealing.

"You should be," she says. "Are we being stupid? Maybe I should just let the farm go. I could find a house in downtown Willowbrook with Mom. I'm sure I can find more graphic design jobs instead of—"

"Sadie, just stop. We're going to be fine."

The word *we* seems odd coming out of me, but that's how it's going to be now. We're a we. My signature on those loan papers means we have to succeed together. Otherwise, we both lose it all.

We venture off Plain Daisy Ranch property and onto hers, and I wonder if this was her plan all along because usually, we stay on our land.

She directs Brownie into a trot through the trees along the small creek that runs through part of their property. When you think about everyone's land around this area, the Wilkinses got screwed in the luck department. They're operating a very small farm. And my dad is right, the soybeans Mr.

Wilkins planted weren't the best option, but what's done is done.

She slows on the other side, and when Brownie stops, Sadie slides her leg over and climbs down. She ties Brownie to the tree, allowing her to get some water and graze. I do the same with Titan, and as always, he finds a way to be as close as he can get to Brownie.

"The best of friends." Sadie smiles and lifts the saddle bag off Brownie. She carries it over to the edge of the drop-off.

"What's in there?" I ask, following her to the lookout that gives a clear view of most of their acreage. Their house sits closest to our property line, along with most of their barns and farm equipment, but this area sits empty.

"You'll see." She holds the saddle bag close to her chest and shoots me a flirty smirk.

"You trying to pay me back for last night?"

I sit on the grass and spread out my legs, taking off my hat and placing it next to us. I'm sweaty and dirty and in desperate need of a shower, but I'd never say no to a ride with Sadie and our horses.

She sits next to me, crossing her legs, and takes some papers out from one side of the saddle bag, placing them on the far side of her. She opens the other side and takes out a carton of ice cream from The Creamery Shoppe. Handing me a spoon, she lifts the lid, revealing their butter brickle ice cream that's my favorite.

"What are you buttering me up for?" I ask, moving my spoon to the ice cream.

She moves the carton away, closer to her chest, teasing me as she moves it back and forth between the two of us. "How bad do you want it?"

"Not that bad." I shrug, playing off as if it means nothing to me.

"I know you better than that. It's been a long, hard day on the ranch herding cattle, and you don't want any ice cream?" She dips her spoon in and slides it into her mouth, exaggerating her moan.

Now it's not the ice cream that I want.

"It's so good, Jude."

She holds it out to me, but I know better than to play her game. It's just like when we'd play the slap hands game. She's always taunted me in more ways than one.

"Nice try." I put my spoon in my mouth and lean back on my hands, tilting my head toward the sun.

She scoffs. "You're no fun." She puts the carton in my lap and lies on the ground, acting upset that I didn't play her game.

I pick up the ice cream and dig my spoon into the vanilla goodness with small pieces of toffee that crunch when I chew them. She knows me way too well. Butter brickle ice cream is my go-to treat after every long day at the ranch.

"Thanks. Hits the spot." She fists blades of grass and tosses them at me, but I twist my torso so it doesn't get in the ice cream. "Hey, now. You carried it all this way, kept it frozen for me, and you're going to ruin it because you're sour?"

She turns to me, shielding her eyes from the sun. "You're lucky I like you so much."

"Ditto."

She turns to the sky again, and I admire her beauty for a second as she's lost in thought.

She sighs. "Are you sure about all this?"

My head rocks back, and I close my eyes for a second. "Jesus, Sadie, stop asking me that. Since when do you know me to do something I don't want to do?"

She sits up and grabs her spoon. I scoot closer to her, and she scoops up a spoonful. "It's still not as good as a tin roof sundae."

She brings her spoon over to take another helping, and I

90

move the carton away. "You can't talk shit about butter brickle and then try to have more."

She giggles and tries again, but I twist my torso again, blocking her. Rising to her knees, she tries to reach it over my shoulders. Quickly, it turns into a cat-and-mouse game. I purposely don't let her have it, and she tries to overpower me. I shelter the small carton under my body, and she jumps on my back, legs straddling me and thrusting her spoon over my shoulder.

"Never going to get it," I taunt.

"Want to make a bet?" she says.

Her tongue slides up the side of my throat, then her teeth bite my earlobe, and not in a sexy way. Regardless, my dick twitches in my jeans as thoughts of swinging her under my body, ditching the ice cream, and devouring her instead jump to the forefront of my mind. Strike that. I'd lather her in ice cream and lick it off one inch at a time.

"So not fair." I get up from under her, needing space before I do something stupid.

"Salt and sweat. Not my best idea." She sticks out her tongue over and over, trying to get rid of the taste.

I hand her the ice cream. "You deserve it."

She smiles and scoops up some ice cream. "Yeah, I do. I see the reason you have three showers a day."

Now that she's on the other side of me, her papers held together with a binder clip are open for me to grab. I pick them up and sit back down as she eats the ice cream next to me. "So, what are these?"

"The plans for the farm."

I thumb through them. She's got everything—the cost of the start-up, what we need to build for the chickens, even a branding page with logos. She always amazes me how she goes all in on something she's committed to.

"It's not complete, but I wanted to make sure you knew that I do not take you doing this for me lightly."

"You know you don't need to show me anything. I'll follow your lead."

She puts the ice cream next to her, and her shoulders sag. "We're both very invested, and I want to work with you on this. I'll need your help and expertise on so many things, and two minds are better than one."

I glance at the papers between us. "What are you asking me?"

She sits up on her knees, taking my hand. "I don't want to do this on my own. I know you have Plain Daisy Ranch and a commitment to your family, but if you're going to marry me, I want you to be a partner in this with me."

"But—"

"Fifty-fifty."

She's right, there's a lot on my plate, but I was ready to help her with whatever she needed, not expecting anything in return. I don't want fifty percent of her profits. But I know her well enough to know she is not going to back down on this.

"Eighty-twenty." And I don't plan on taking my twenty.

"Jude..." she says with exhaustion in her tone.

"Sadie..." I mimic her tone.

Her straight back and glare say she's not going to argue this point.

"Fine." I put out my hand between us. I'll never take my fifty percent, and if she forces it, I'll find some way of getting it back to her.

"Thank you." She tackles me to the ground and hugs me. "You're the best friend a girl could ask for."

My hands fall to her hips. She's so close, the tip of her braid is touching my cheek. Our eyes meet and lock for a blink of an eye as my body registers the heat and the weight of hers on top of me.

She scurries off me. "Sorry, I should've just shaken your hand."

"If you want to pay me with hugs or more, I'm game."

She shoves me and grabs the ice cream.

I sit next to her and grab my spoon, and we ignore the tension between us, devoting our full attention to the ice cream while the sun sets. I'm pretty sure I've taken my horse down an unbeaten path by asking Sadie to marry me. It's too late to turn around now though.

Chapter Eleven

SADIE

"Maybe you'd be better off if you went on your own." Jude climbs out of his truck.

He's freshly showered with a spritz of cologne, hair perfectly styled with no hat to be found, although his hair still has that messy look I love on him. He's been telling me the entire drive over here that my mom is going to see right through him.

"Oh, stop it. She loves you." I join him at the front of his truck and take his hand. He glances down and back up at me. "We're supposed to be in love. You just proposed."

He nods. "Yeah, of course."

He steps forward, leading me by the hand up my mom's porch steps. Once we're at the door, Jude stops, and I'm not sure why. The man has been walking into my family's house for years. Usually, he gives a short knock, then he peeks his head in.

It's as if with the ring on my left hand, his mind is overloaded, and he can't figure out how to act around me.

"Mom?" I open the screen door.

"Up here. I'll be right down."

"Okay." I head into the small kitchen. "Want something to drink?" I shout to Jude.

"Sure," he says from the door frame. He's leaning his body along it, his hands stuffed into his pockets.

"What are you doing?" I grab two pops from the fridge and hand him one.

"Don't couples stick together all the time?"

I laugh, but Jude doesn't. Sometimes I forget he never grew up with an example of a couple since his mom died so young. But I'm not sure if he's being sarcastic or not.

"I think they might not follow each other to the bathroom," I say, and he chuckles, signaling he was, in fact, joking.

"I'm nervous," he admits. "I hate lying."

I put my finger over his mouth, but the stair creaks will tell us when my mom is on her way down. "Shh..."

He opens his mouth and bites my finger.

"Ouch." I pull it back.

"That's payback for licking my neck the other day."

"I'll give you that one." I walk by him, and our bodies brush against each other. Those dreaded butterflies take flight in my stomach.

Thankfully, they die quickly with the sound of the stairs creaking. My mom appears right before I sit on the couch.

Jude waits at the end of the staircase, offering my mom his hand. "Hi, Mrs. Wilkins."

"Jude. How sweet." She puts her hand in his and eases off the last step. She'll need to either move into a room downstairs soon, or we'll have to figure something out with the stairs. "What brings you two over?"

Jude escorts her to her recliner, then he sits down next to me.

"We have something to tell you," I say, my nerves causing my words to shake.

"Oh." Her eyes fall to the space between us on the couch.

Jude is really bad at this pretend stuff.

I take his hand, but he doesn't scoot closer.

"Oh look, I love this game." Her attention goes to the television.

I take the opportunity to get Jude to move closer. I glare at the space between us and look at him, but his eyes are on the television.

"She should have asked for an R," he says.

"How about a T?" My mom shakes her head. As usual, she believes she'd be an ace at the game. The contestants aren't very bright, according to her.

I knock Jude's leg with our adjoined hands. He looks down, and his eyes meet mine. He mouths, what? I look at the space between us again, and he shrugs.

"Oh, for heaven's sake, she's paying for a vowel." Mom shakes her head.

I mouth for him to move over, and he nods as if two live wires just connected inside his head. He slides over, and my body zings with awareness when our thighs touch.

"Mom," I say, wanting to get this over with.

"Yes, sweetie," she says, not looking my way.

"We have something to tell you."

"What's that? Oh, Jude, did you see he was on a roll, and now he's bankrupt? Poor luck."

"Mom," I repeat, hoping to grab her attention before the commercials come on.

"What?" She looks over, and this time she zeros in on our linked hands resting on my leg. "Oh." She leans back and grabs the remote, muting the television.

I slide my hand out from Jude's and lift my left hand. "Jude asked me to marry him."

She stares at the ring on my hand then at Jude. "You proposed?"

Jude fidgets.

"I know it's out of the blue, but—" I start to say.

"I should've asked you. I'm sorry, Mrs. Wilkins. It was kind of impromptu. Please forgive me."

I turn my head toward Jude, surprised by the sincerity in his voice. Once we're done with this marriage of convenience, I know he'll find his real wife and ask her family for her hand in marriage. I push that thought from my mind because it feels as if my dinner is about to come up.

"It's okay. I think Monty..." Mom doesn't finish the sentence, waving.

"What?" I ask, forehead wrinkling.

"Nothing, sweetie. Just your dad would have said yes to Jude. He always viewed you like a son, but..." She stops.

I prepare myself to answer a barrage of questions. Last night, I went over what I suspect she'll ask and prepped every answer I could.

"We've been keeping it from you, and I'm sorry. We just didn't want the pressure of people's expectations until we knew for certain." I tell her our excuse for hiding a relationship we've supposedly been in, hoping she'll buy it.

"So, this isn't because of the farm?" I should've known my mom would ask directly.

"No, Mrs. Wilkins." He grabs my hand, linking our fingers without the ease of a couple in love, but I'll take it for today because my mom smiles. "I love your daughter."

There's so much conviction in Jude's words, wetness pools in my eyes, but I push it back. *Get it together, Sadie.*

"I know you love her, Jude. But are you *in* love with her?"

God, Mom. I see now why Jude didn't want to come.

"Mom," I plead, desperate to save Jude because he is the worst liar. I'll never understand how he got this over on his dad.

"Shh, Sadie. The question is for Jude."

Jude doesn't say anything for what I swear is an entire

minute, and the anxiety filling my veins rushes to my heart. She's going to call us out. I just know it.

"Mrs. Wilkins, I would never ask Sadie to marry me if I wasn't in love with her. You have my word." Jude brings our joined hands to his lips, kissing the top of my hand. "I feel lucky to have my best friend be my wife."

The air whooshes from my lungs. Whether from relief at his answer or because of how sincere he sounds and how it makes me feel, I can't be sure.

My mom's smile grows wider, and she looks at me, her expression filled with love. "I'm so happy to hear that. Oh, I wish Monty were here. He always said..." She waves again, reaching for a tissue and blotting her eyes.

Did we really just pull this off?

She quickly lowers the tissue, and through the remaining tears trickling down her cheeks, she says, "So, what are you thinking? We have to get you a dress, and oh, there's so much to do. When are you thinking? A year? A year and a half? We can go to Lincoln to find a dress and—"

I hate to do this to her. She's probably dreamed about my wedding as long as I have. "We're thinking small. At The Knotted Barn. And I'm just going to get something shipped in. No need to make a lot of fuss."

My mom's hand with the tissue lowers, and her eyes lock on mine. All her unanswered questions rest there in her green hues. The guilt burrows deeper inside me.

"Oh. I figured...I mean, you always wanted a big wedding."

"I..." I look to Jude for him to jump in here. I'm breaking my mom's heart, and I'm one more assumption from telling her the truth.

"We don't want to waste a lot of time," he says, attempting the save, causing my mom's back to straighten.

"Why?" The tears dry up fast, and she lasers in on me for

an answer. "Why are you in such a rush? It's because of the farm, isn't it?" She shakes her head. "No way, you two."

"No, what?" I ask.

"You both need to let this farm go."

"It has nothing to do with the farm." I turn to Jude, widening my eyes so he backs me up.

He clears his throat. "Mrs. Wilkins, we don't want to wait another year. We've already waited so long, that's all."

Holy shit, I'm starting to think Jude actually can lie. Where did that come from?

"Really?" my mom asks, looking between us. "I suppose, if anything, your dad's passing made it clear how fast things can change."

Jude slides his hand from mine and wraps it around my waist, tucking me into his side. This is something we've never done, and my cheeks heat from feeling like a real couple. "Yes."

She stares long and hard at us.

Jude's hand slides up to my shoulder to the side of my head, and he leans over, kissing my cheek. "I'll be right back. I have to use the bathroom."

What? He's leaving me? But my mom's eyes stay on the cheek that he just kissed, so I think he might have helped our case.

"Okay," I say, inflecting in my tone that he's leaving me high and dry.

He walks through the kitchen toward the bathroom.

"Sadie?" From my mom's tone, I know she's asking me to tell her the truth.

God, this is killing me, but she'd never allow me to go through with the wedding if she knew the reason why, and she has enough to deal with right now.

"I love him, Mom." It's not a lie. I do love Jude. It's only the whole marriage part that's the lie.

"I know, sweetie. Are you sure?"

I nod. "Yes, Mom."

"Well, you're an adult. I can't stop you. I wish your dad were here." That causes a pinch in my chest. She leans closer, lowering her voice. "He always thought Jude was the one for you. He told me he spoke to Jude once—"

"We're gonna be late, Sadie," Jude says, interrupting. "We're going to the football game," he says to my mom.

My mom winks at me, straightening in her chair.

I'd really like her to finish that sentence. She alluded earlier to my dad talking to Jude and now again.

"What a great night," she says. "I'll have to make it to one one of these days. I heard Gillian's boy is really good."

"Yeah." Jude stands there with his hands in his pockets. "He'll probably follow in Ben's footsteps. He'll play in college at the very least."

"That's great. You two go." She waves me off and winks again.

I'm unsure if our conversation is over or not, but I guess there isn't much else to say.

"Maybe we can have Bruce over and talk logistics," my mom suggests.

Yeah, I'll be handling it all and telling my mom what needs to happen because there's no way I can see her sadness at not hosting the big wedding we used to talk about all the time and not having my dad here for it.

"We'll see. We're going to talk to Romy about when we can get The Knotted Barn and go from there." I kiss her cheek. "Bye, Mom."

"Bye, sweetie."

Jude walks over and kisses her cheek. She whispers something to him, and his smile falters before he draws back. It reemerges, but it's not Jude's usual smile. It's his forced and fake one. A lot of people don't notice the difference. It's hard to tell, but his lips don't tip as high, and he doesn't show his teeth.

"Go Wildcats!" Mom puts up her arm, then grabs the remote.

We say one more goodbye and walk out of the house. Jude walks me to the passenger side of his truck, opens the door for me, and I climb in. He closes my door, rounds the front of the truck, and gets into the driver's seat.

"What did she say?" I ask.

No smile creases his lips anymore. He doesn't look at me, just starts his truck. "She just said she was happy for us."

For the first time tonight, Jude's inability to lie shines bright. As convincing as he was to my mom, he just lied to me. But the question is why? What am I missing?

Chapter Twelve

JUDE

I park my truck in the high school parking lot. The lights on the football field I used to play on light up the night. The sun had set in the time we drove here from Sadie's. I'm relieved that both our parents know about our engagement and didn't question us to the point that we broke. Mrs. Wilkins seemed to suspect something, but she didn't push.

The worst part about telling Sadie's mom was how excited she was to plan the wedding and buy Sadie's dress. That about killed me, and I'm sure Sadie felt the same way.

I turn off the engine and look at Sadie.

All the Wildcat fans are parking and walking toward the entrance of the football stadium. This is the second part of our plan. Announcing us as a couple to the town of Willowbrook since almost no one misses a game. Once we do this, there's no going back.

"This is it. We'll hold hands. I'll pay for you to get in." It feels hard to speak, as though someone has a grip on my neck or something, and I clear my throat.

"You pay for me every time," she says, smiling.

Sadie trusts that everyone sees the good in people, just like she does. But there will be people studying us tonight, looking for signs that we're fake.

"We'll go up to the bleachers and sit by one another."

"You realize the only difference will be the hand holding, right? Everything else is what we do every game." She unbuckles herself and grabs her purse. "Let's just play it by ear."

I lightly take her arm to stop her from exiting the truck. "If we play it by ear, we're going to mess it up."

She twists back around to face me, her purse snug in her lap. "Okay then. How about we make out? Oh, do you want to go under the bleachers like the high schoolers? Make a real show of it?"

"Sadie." I rest my forehead on my steering wheel. "This is serious."

"I am serious. Rumors will fly if we're tongue-tied under the bleachers."

"Why don't I just lay you down at the fifty-yard line during half time then?"

She snaps her fingers. "Perfect. You're so smart."

"Jesus, Sadie." I open the truck door and climb out, shutting it.

She's already at the back of my truck by the time I get there. Her hands land on my cheeks, and she rises onto her tiptoes. "Relax. I'll act all smitten, and you just have to touch me a lot."

"I'm not a touchy guy," I remind her.

She knows me well enough. Just holding her hand at her mom's house earlier felt weird. Then again, over the years I have grown to love Sadie's hugs. She fits perfectly in my arms, as though she's meant to be there, and for a brief moment, I always forget she's not mine.

She slides her hand into mine and pulls me forward. "Tonight, you are."

I allow her to drag me, and I fall in line with her, tightening my hold on her soft skin and delicate fingers. "No one would believe that I'd let you lead the way."

"Excuse me? Lead the way?" She stops just before we get to the gate. "Plenty of people would believe it if I was to drag you in, kicking and screaming, while holding your hand. Willowbrook knows you keep your emotions closed off."

She has a point. If this was real, how would I really act? Probably hold her hand. Probably buy her popcorn. But I probably wouldn't kiss her. Nor would I get all cuddly with her in front of everyone. I'm not a fan of public displays of affection. Ben is all over Gillian all the fucking time, and I have no idea why he'd want to share that with everyone and their mother. That's Ben, not me.

"We just have to be a tad more affectionate than we usually are. You might have to whisper in my ear, and I'll laugh like you're the next up-and-coming comedian on *Saturday Night Live*."

"I'm funny." I'm starting to get a complex with some of the shit she's saying these days.

"You're hilarious. To me. *With* me. But not everyone sees that side of you. Come on. People are side-eyeing us already." She walks ahead.

I grab her hand, linking our fingers tightly. "That's a good thing. We'll draw their attention as if we're unsure how to come out."

We reach the gate, and I pull out my wallet to pay for our admission.

"How are you guys? Almost missed kickoff," Alondra, the president of the booster club, says as she takes my cash. She's fishing for information. Always is.

"Had a hard time leaving my house tonight." I wink, and Alondra turns to look at her sidekick, Tori, as if asking her if she heard me correctly.

Sadie slides her arm through mine and gets closer. When her breast brushes along my arm, my jaw tightens. Her hand runs up and down my arm. "Jude made me dinner."

"Oh, how sweet," Alondra says.

"What did he make?" Tori interrupts, pushing into our conversation.

"Salmon and my favorite garlic mashed potatoes." Sadie refers to the meal I made the other night. Weaving truth with the lie. Smart.

"Don't forget the green beans," I say, and Sadie leans her head on my bicep.

"How could I? My favorite. See, Jude's an asparagus guy, but he made my favorite instead." Her hand keeps running up and down my arm, but neither nosy woman says anything.

"You're finally here." Lottie makes her way over from the concession stand. She's got a tray full of food—pizza, nachos, popcorn, and a drink. Plus, a candy bar.

How does this woman survive on junk food?

"Stop judging. It's my one cheat day a week." She holds her tray with one hand and uses the other to dip a chip in the nacho cheese and eat it. She stops right next to Alondra. "Did you hear that my cousin finally got his head out of his ass?"

"I thought I noticed a ring," Alondra says.

Sadie holds up her left hand. "Oh, I forgot that we haven't told many people."

Alondra smiles, but it doesn't reach her eyes. I've never been sought after like Ben, but I've had my fair share of numbers slipped to me at The Hidden Cave.

"So...you two are engaged?" She waves her finger back and forth between us.

"Yep!" Sadie says and eyes Lottie.

"Just the other night. She rushed over to tell me. Now we're finally going to be best friends *and* family!" Lottie sells our situation better than either of us. "Come on, guys, you're holding up the line."

I look over my shoulder. Sure enough, a line is forming, but most of them seem as though they're listening to our conversation. Each one probably wants to be the first one to tell their friends and make sure they know that they knew the gossip first.

"Thanks for the save," I say as Sadie tucks her hand into mine again on the way to the stands.

"So, how was it with the parents?" Lottie whispers as Sadie snags a chip.

"Everyone is on board," Sadie says before placing the chip in her mouth.

We walk up the bleachers and head in the direction to where my family usually sits.

"Heard a rumor!" Emmett pops up behind us.

Sadie yelps.

"Fucking hell." I glare at him.

He holds up his hands. "You can't blame me when Sadie waves her diamond ring to the booster women. You two are the talk of the entry line now."

"So annoying," Sadie says and rolls her eyes, leaving me to accompany Lottie to our seats.

Emmett claps me on the shoulder. "So, that's it, huh?" His eyebrows raise slightly indicating he knows why we're doing it.

"It's real, Emmett," I say.

"Sure, it is. I love Sadie, and I love the fact I get another sister-in-law. Way to man up."

I roll my eyes. "Right, thanks."

"Sadie Wilkins!" a woman shouts, interrupting Emmett and me.

I look up to see Gillian and my cousin, Romy, weaving through the crowd to reach Sadie. They gush over her, lifting her hand and hugging her. Everyone else around rushes her, congratulating her too.

Yes, this is definitely the best place for our grand coming out.

"Good thing there isn't a kiss cam here, huh?" Emmett slaps me on the back and bounds up the stairs, picking up Sadie and swinging her around.

I stuff my hands in my pockets and watch Sadie's smile grow. A part of me wishes this was real for her because I know how much she wants a big wedding and a big fuss.

A few people who heard the commotion congratulate me as I walk up the stairs, and I nod my thanks to them. By the time I reach my family, everyone is sitting. Gillian gets up so I can sit next to Sadie.

Sadie puts her hand on my thigh, and I rest my arm around her back. We watch Ben coach the varsity high school team. He's doing a great job, and I'm happy to have him back in Willowbrook after he retired from the pros.

At the half, we're winning by one touchdown. When the pom squad comes onto the field doing their dance, a few people leave the stands to get food and use the bathroom. I'm counting down the minutes until the game is over, and we can get the hell out of here. I feel like a damn zoo animal with all the eyes on us, watching and assessing.

"Let's hear it for the Wildcat Pom Squad," the announcer in the booth says over the speakers, and everyone claps and cheers.

Sadie leans over to me and whispers, "You need to up your game, Mister Stoic."

I shift our positions so I'm talking directly in her ear. "This is me in a relationship."

"Then I pity myself," she says, drawing back and exaggerating her frown.

"And lastly, rumor is that Jude Noughton and Sadie

Wilkins are engaged. Who knew? Not me." The announcer plays the wedding march song, and everyone around us turns to face us. Every pair of eyes, even the players as they run back onto the field, seek us out. "Stand up, you two. We've been waiting forever for this day."

I groan and roll my eyes.

"Jude and Sadie!" Emmett chants and claps over and over, urging the rest of the crowd to do the same.

"Kiss her!" I hear someone scream. I swear it was Brooks. Shouldn't he be doing some sheriff shit or something?

The announcer starts saying, "Kiss her!"

Soon the entire high school stadium is chanting it.

"Come on, guys." Lottie urges us with her hand and gives us a stern look.

I reluctantly stand and hold my hand out to Sadie. She rises to her feet, and I wrap my arms around her waist. She steps into me, and I tuck her in tighter. Her tongue slides out and wets her lips.

This isn't something I want to do in public. Kissing Sadie for the first time in my life in front of our entire town sounds like a special sort of hell. I've long imagined what it might be like to kiss this woman, but it was never like this. But I guess I'll have to kiss her at our wedding, so this is like practice.

She pushes up on her tiptoes, and I bend my head to reach her. We come together, our lips moments from meeting, and a part of me is excited to finally know how she tastes, how her lips feel against mine, even if everyone is watching. My hand slides just under her shirt, feeling the smooth skin on her lower back, and I dip lower, eager to kiss her now, with or without the audience.

We're millimeters apart, and the entire stadium quiets, or at least I can't hear them. At the last second, Sadie turns her head, and my lips land on her cheek. Everyone boos. I find myself wanting to join them because we were so close.

"Wait until the wedding!" she shouts at everyone, and they continue to boo.

"I guess back to the game, Wildcats," the announcer says.

I sit back down on the bleachers and watch the game, confused as to why she didn't try to sell us, but I think I'm mostly upset because I really wanted to kiss her.

Jesus, we haven't made it down the aisle and already things are getting confusing. Not a good sign.

Chapter Thirteen

SADIE

I stop at Jude's during his lunch hour so we can meet with Romy at The Knotted Barn and figure out what day we can get married. I'd like it to be as soon as possible, before my nerves get the better of me, and so I can get the loan cosigned and make sure the farm isn't sold.

"Are you ready?" I shout, walking in through the screen door.

He jogs down his stairs, freshly showered and dressed in a clean shirt and jeans. "I just have to grab my wallet."

I swing my keys around my finger. "Great. I'll drive."

He goes to the small table by the front door, slides on his cowboy boots, and pockets his wallet. "I was thinking we'd take the UTV."

"Oh, I figured you had to get back right after." I stand by the door, waiting for him.

He opens the drawer in his table and pulls out the keys to his UTV. "Dad's taking Emmett today. Said we need to get this wedding going."

He steps over to me and waits for me to go out the door

first, then he shuts his front door, and we both bound down the steps.

"Do you find it weird that we haven't gotten a lot of questions about the validity of our engagement?" I ask on the way to his garage, which holds the UTV.

It's a four-seater that Jude uses a lot when he wants to get around the grounds of Plain Daisy Ranch faster than he can on horseback.

"I'm not questioning it. It's probably because it goes along with the narrative everyone's always spewing that we've been secretly seeing one another our entire lives."

I slide into the passenger seat. "I guess, but your dad didn't say anything?"

"Just that we couldn't elope."

He starts the UTV and drives with one hand on the wheel, heading down the path that goes around the lake. Their land is expansive and pretty with grown adult trees that shade the drive.

"You clean up nice," I say, unable to stop myself.

He glances over, and one side of his lips tip into a smirk. "Thanks. Same to you."

The breeze flows through my hair, and I hold it at the side of my neck so it won't blow in my face.

We arrive at The Knotted Barn not too long after. It sits on a hill and overlooks the winery Jude's uncle started years ago. There was lots of talk in town when that happened. People were judgmental and mean, saying that the grape vines would never survive, but now they bottle two varieties a year and have a regular customer base.

We climb out of the UTV, and Jude reaches for my hand without me having to remind him. After the near-kiss at the football game the other night, I worried I'd hurt our case. I was desperate to kiss him, but I didn't want to kiss Jude for the first time in front of everyone in town. Sure, the wedding will probably be our first kiss, which sucks too, but better that than a football game.

"You're learning fast," I say and raise our entwined hands.

He glances over. "I have a really good teacher. Even though the teacher gave me her cheek."

"Yeah, I told you, it felt weird with everyone watching."

He nods and doesn't say anything. As usual, Jude keeps all his emotions held tighter than a vise.

We walk into The Knotted Barn, the door shutting behind us. A few workers are setting dishes on the tables, and music plays in the background. Jude weaves us through to Romy's office in the back hallway, and we find her sitting behind her desk.

She smiles when she notices us. She signals with her hand for us to sit in the two chairs opposite her desk. "Who would've bet on this day happening?"

"Was there a bet?" Jude asks.

Romy smiles sweetly and doesn't answer the question. The Noughton cousins are known for betting on anything and everything, especially when it comes to their cousins' personal lives.

"So, I got the best news today. Well, not good news for everyone." She cringes. "There was a wedding booked in two weeks, but the groom found the bride with the best man."

"Seriously? That's a country song." I inch up on the edge of my chair.

"I know, but it's not the first time. But the good news is that you guys can have the date. I'd never fill that spot with such short notice, and you said you wanted to get married fast, right?"

I lay my hand over Jude's on the arm rest. "Yes."

"Sooner the better," Jude chimes in.

Romy stares at her cousin for an extra-long beat, and I worry she can tell something is off, but she turns her attention to her computer, and her fingers click on the keyboard. "Great. So, we could do this one of two ways."

Jude clears his throat. "It's just a wedding, Romy. We say I do, and it's over."

"Well, that's romantic, Jude. How about you think of your bride here?" Romy rolls her eyes. She shifts her position from behind the computer to face us.

"What are the two options?" I ask.

"We could just do the wedding and reception, but the couple who canceled had decided on a package deal, so that's all available to you if you like."

"A package?" Jude asks.

Romy sets her gaze on me. "They were from Hickory. Sometimes our couples come and stay a few weekends to get all the planning done, and I see now why they never made the trip. Clearly someone wasn't interested in planning. But the appointments for them have been made, so if you want to take their place, you can."

"Appointments for what?" Jude asks, and I squeeze his hand until he slides it out from under me.

"I'm curious—what do you think planning a wedding entails, Jude?" Romy asks, straightening her back and clasping her hands on her desk. She's clearly insulted by his insinuation that a wedding is a ceremony and a meal and easy to pull off.

"I get that we need a cake, but Laurel will bake that up," Jude says. "And I don't need to try a menu from Jensen. I can tell you what Sadie and I like that he cooks. At Gillian's law school graduation party, he made those cheese puff pastries. I liked those."

Romy scoffs. "Okay. It's not just *I do*, cake, and puff pastries." She turns her attention back to me. "You do the cake

114

tasting, you get a dance lesson, and you meet with the DJ to pick out your songs, and lastly, this one is my favorite."

"What is it?" I rack my brain to think of what could be missing.

"A tantric yoga session and a meeting with a sex therapist." She claps her hands softly, and my gut feels like an ocean liner sinking to the bottom.

"Yoga? Sex therapist?" Jude's facial expression says that's about the last thing he wants to do. Which of course it is. This is Jude we're talking about.

"Yes. Open up your mind. It can be amazing and so spiritual."

"Yeah, no. We don't need that, right?" he asks me.

I'm sure normal brides would push their grooms to do it. But we're not a normal bride and groom. What's the right call here? "Um..."

"See, Jude, she wants to do it. Are you really going to deny her?"

"You want to do it?" Jude asks me, eyes wide.

"I don't know. A lot of couples do it?" I ask Romy.

"Sure, most of the grooms agree." She shoots Jude a death glare. "Some argue about it, but the bride can usually convince her man." She looks at Jude again with the same glare. "Enjoy it. It's very sexual, and I assure you, you'll probably get lucky afterward." She winks.

Well, that's not going to happen.

"Fine," Jude says with the enthusiasm of a toddler eating their peas.

"Great. I'll mark you down." Romy's smile is a little too wide. I think she's just pushing it to force her cousin to do something he doesn't want to.

"When is the actual wedding date?" I ask.

"Oh, yeah. It's a Sunday actually—not this one, but the

next. I'll set up all your appointments, and you just have to show up. It's all taken care of."

"We should pay for the time," I say.

"No, we shouldn't," Jude chimes in with a frown.

My head whips in his direction. "Why not?"

"Because we're Noughtons."

The words we're and Noughtons are odd coming from Jude's lips, but I can't deny that I like the sound of it. How many times did I write Sadie Noughton or Mrs. Jude Noughton throughout the years when I was doodling?

"Yeah, I would never charge you. Plus, the deposit they paid is plenty to cover the appointments. I'm just happy we were able to squeeze you guys in. Since you're in a rush and all." Her eyes stay trained on me.

I force a convincing smile, hoping to slip this facade by another person. "Well thank you, Romy. We really appreciate it, right, Jude?"

He doesn't say much, his eyes on the pictures of happy brides and grooms on the office wall. I kick him, and he looks at us.

"Yeah," he says, not knowing what he's agreeing to.

"I'll be in touch, and if there's anything you really want to incorporate into the wedding, let me know." Romy smiles and stands from behind her desk.

"We're fine with whatever you usually do. Neither of us is picky," I say, standing as well.

Jude is still sitting there staring at the pictures of couples kissing on the balcony as the sun sets. At least we're getting married at a beautiful place.

"You should be picky. It's your wedding. Do what you want." Romy rounds the desk and opens her arms to hug me.

Jude finally stands, and he and Romy give each other a one-arm hug. "Thanks, Romy."

"Anything for family." She walks us out but gets distracted

by directing the employees to do something. "I'll catch you two later. Congratulations!"

She waves, and we wave back before walking out the doors.

"Tantric yoga? What the hell is that?" Jude walks toward the UTV.

"There's something called the internet. Look it up." I slide into the seat beside him, and he revs up the UTV. Maybe this is getting too real for him. "We don't have to do it."

"If most couples do it, we should too."

I'm surprised that Jude isn't taking on his usual attitude of "who gives a shit what people think." He's putting forth a lot of effort to make this look real.

"Okay. Well, if you get uncomfortable, we can cut it short."

He stops at the bridge that crosses the river by Ben's house. "Don't worry about me. Whatever you want, Sadie, ask for it. This is your wedding."

He presses on the gas, and I sit there silently because if I told him what I really want, it would be him. I care about a wedding, but at this point, I would be happy to have Jude be more than just my friend. But I need to concentrate on getting this chicken farm off the ground, and I can't risk changing our dynamic and messing that up.

"Everything she suggested is fine." I cross my legs and let the wind run through my hair.

He pulls into his garage, and I climb out, ready to go to my car.

"Stay," he says.

"You have to get back to work."

Jude shakes his head. "Dad gave me the afternoon off. How about we put the wedding aside and talk chicken farm?"

I smile and walk over to him. "Sure."

"I was looking through your plans..."

We go up to his porch and into his house, where I find all

the papers I gave him on the coffee table. I must have been distracted earlier by him coming down the stairs just out of the shower. We grab some drinks and chips and salsa, sitting down to go through our to-do list in priority order.

Yeah, I might not be marrying him because he loves me, but I'm still marrying one hell of a man.

Chapter Fourteen

JUDE

The first thing on the agenda is the cake tasting, which I'm not complaining about.

I park my truck downtown and sit to wait for her. I'm meeting Sadie here since she went to a farm a county over to see their chicken farm and get more information. I'm not a small talk kind of guy, so rather than go inside the bakery and wait for Sadie there, I look up tantric yoga on my phone.

Fuck. My body doesn't bend like the people in this video. It's going to be a disaster.

A bang on my window almost makes my heart stop in my chest.

"Fucking hell." I roll down the window to speak to Ben.

"Why are you watching porn in your truck?" he asks.

"I'm waiting for Sadie. And I'm not watching porn. Go away."

"Since my fiancée got dragged here this morning to help Laurel with your wedding cake, you can keep me busy until Sadie gets here."

"You do know that the two of you aren't conjoined twins? You can do things separately, right?"

"Sundays are our days together." He opens my door and waits for me to step out.

I groan and unbuckle myself, turning off the truck and climbing out. "Happy?"

"Ecstatic. We haven't had any brother time since Dad kicked me out. I must say, I was pissed he did, but living with Gillian at her place isn't anything to complain about. Morning sex, nooners, sex every night. Hell, Clayton went to his buddy's house and the blowjob—"

"You sound like Emmett. I don't need to hear your sex stories."

In truth, Ben isn't usually a guy who kisses and tells, so I'm a bit surprised he's telling me this. I think there's an ulterior motive, but I'm not sure what it would be.

"Just trying to tell you what you're missing out on. Move Sadie in."

There it is. She and I haven't even discussed when that will happen, which is odd since I put together the whole plan to let people know we're a couple. I guess I should put that on the agenda. "She's got her mom to worry about."

"She's not going to be that far away if her mom needs her. And you're getting married soon anyway."

I take off my baseball hat and run my hand through my hair. "Still. After the wedding."

He nods and gives me the look that says there's a list of questions running through his brain.

"What?" I say, exhausted.

"Are you marrying her because of Dad?" He looks around the sidewalk, but it's after the breakfast rush in the morning, so not a lot of people are milling about. "I mean, it happened so fast. I won't tell anyone. Not even Emmett."

"No. I just..." It's hard not to tell Ben. Sadie has Lottie to talk to.

"Actually." He holds up a hand. "Don't tell me. Because if

you tell me, then I have to tell Gillian, and I think she'd keep it a secret, but I can't honor the brother code on this one. I'd have to tell her."

But I really want to ask for his advice. Am I making a big mistake? Could I ruin my friendship with Sadie if this goes south? That's what I've been trying to avoid all these years that I've been pining away for her and not saying anything. Am I about to do it now in a different way? She deserves the world, and I don't want to stop her from having it.

It doesn't matter, though. We're too far into this. Plus, it's Sadie. She's my best friend and deserves this opportunity.

Thankfully, Sadie pulls up and parks next to my truck, giving me an out from this conversation with Ben.

"Hey, I have something to talk to you about later," Ben whispers.

"What is it?" I watch Sadie get out of her car. It was her grandma's, and she won't get rid of it. I'd like her in something a lot more reliable in the winter, but she fights me every year when I bring it up.

"Briar."

"Gillian's sister?" I wonder why he has to talk to me about Briar but doesn't want to do it in front of Sadie.

"Yeah. She might be returning to Willowbrook."

"And?"

"Hey, you two. Why are you waiting outside? Ben, are you sampling with us?" She walks right by the two of us and holds open the door of Laurel's bakery.

"I'm gonna get some type of sugar since you're the reason I'm not in bed with Gillian right now."

I slap him in the stomach with the back of my hand.

"You'll understand when you're getting regular sex and someone cockblocks you—a.k.a., cake tasting." He walks in past Sadie.

"Keep up with the way you do it, and there's going to be a dozen little Bens running around," Sadie says to his back.

He turns around. "Do you two need a lesson on birth control before your nuptials?"

"Fuck off," I say, flipping him off, and he laughs, walking back into the kitchen.

"Well then." Sadie stops by the glass case.

"How was the farm?" I ask.

"Oh, I can't wait to tell you everything they told me, and I don't think it's going to cost a crazy amount."

"Perfect."

"Hey, you two, you don't get the formality everyone else does," Laurel calls from the back. "Get your asses back in the kitchen."

We walk back there, and Gillian rushes over to hug Sadie then me. "I can't wait to see what you decide on."

"I feel like we're stepping on your toes," Sadie says to her, eyes full of concern.

"Why?" I ask, not following.

Gillian holds up her left hand with her sizable diamond ring from Ben. Damn, I should've gone bigger. "Because your brother proposed first."

"Yeah, asshole, you're stealing our thunder." Ben's smile says he doesn't give a shit.

Gillian tilts her head and sighs. "No, you're not. We couldn't be happier for you guys."

"I'm older, so technically I should be married first," I say and rock back on my heels.

"But you're about a decade too late," Ben says.

"I could say the same." I arch an eyebrow at him.

"Okay, brothers, retreat to your separate corners." Laurel puts out her hands. "Sadie and Jude, your cake tasting." She widens her arms over the stainless-steel table between us.

I'm not gonna lie, I fucking love this task on the wedding

agenda. I sit on a stool next to Sadie and stare at all the different varieties of cake.

"You outdid yourself, Laurel. I'm not picky." Sadie grabs the closest plate with two small forks next to it.

"That's the classic chocolate with raspberry filling and a whipped cream."

I fork a piece of cake, ready to eat it.

"Oh no, no, no. You should practice for the big day," Ben says.

I stop with the fork halfway to my mouth and glare at him from the corner of my eye.

"It's a cake tasting," Sadie says. Thank god she doesn't want to entertain this stupid idea of my younger brother's.

"Oh, that would be fun. Feed each other." Gillian motions with her hands as if we're kindergarteners who need her to explain it to us.

I look to Sadie for her to make the decision, and she shrugs.

"Come on. This way you won't mess up at the wedding. No bride wants cake on her face," Laurel chimes in with her two cents I'd rather not hear.

"I guess." Sadie moves her arm around mine.

"Mind if I snap a pic?" Ben asks, pulling out his phone.

I give him a look. "You take that phone out, and I'll throw it in the mixer."

"Memories," Ben says with a shit-eating grin.

"You're taking a picture for Emmett, asshole."

"And Brooks." Ben shrugs as though I should've known that.

"You can take it at the wedding," Sadie says.

I hold the fork out toward her, and I feel fucking lame. Sadie laughs right before she opens her mouth for me to slide the fork in, and I miss her mouth, getting whipped cream on the side of her lips. She gets her fork in my mouth perfectly. Of course I fuck it up.

The cake tastes great. What's not to love with cake? But raspberry isn't my thing.

"Oh, Sadie, you have a little whipped cream." Laurel grabs a napkin and hands it to me to hand to Sadie since I'm closest.

"That's not how you get whipped cream off the woman you love." Ben laughs.

"Ben, shut the fuck up."

He shrugs. "I'd lick it off Gillian."

"Since you practically hump her every time you're around her, I'm not surprised."

Sadie reaches for the napkin.

"At least use your finger, Jude," my future sister-in-law says.

Okay, I'd like Ben and Gillian to leave now.

Not wanting to hear any more shit and to keep up the charade, I ditch the napkin and swipe my finger on the corner of her mouth. But Sadie doesn't realize I'm going to do it and slides her tongue out to get it right as my finger lands there, so she licks the whipped cream off the tip of my finger.

My dick twitches, my jeans suddenly getting tight. Holy shit.

"There you go," Ben says. "He's a slow learner, Sadie, way to take the reins."

I'm not even paying attention to Ben because her tongue on my finger instantly makes me think about her mouth wrapped around my dick. Which is the last thought I need right now.

"Should we all leave?" Gillian asks in jest.

My eyes lock with Sadie's, and I'm sure my cheeks are as red as hers. I gulp to get a hold of myself.

"What else do you have, Laurel?" Sadie asks. I'm slightly irked that she's able to recover so quickly.

"Red velvet and cream cheese frosting. The most popular." She slides it past me, and I pick up a fork.

"Don't miss this time," Ben eggs me on, and I grind my teeth.

I don't miss with any of the eight other cake variations we try. By the last one, I never want to see cake again.

We ultimately decide to have three different tiers. Chocolate on chocolate, vanilla bean with a buttercream, and a red velvet. The cakes will be scattered instead of stacked, each one decorated with a lace pattern Sadie picked out. If she's getting one thing she would've picked out for her real wedding, it's the cake, which makes both of us happy.

And all I ever want is for Sadie to be happy.

Chapter Fifteen

SADIE

So far, we've completed all the items in Romy's package. We did the dance lesson last night, which thrilled Jude about as much as having a tooth extracted. What started as a disaster with us stepping all over each other's toes turned out pretty well in the end. Unless you consider that the nearness of having him so close and having his hand on the small of my back, where he'd rub his thumb up and down, made sparks of electricity pulsate through my body. This charade is making me want him more, which isn't great. I need to keep my eye on the prize—my family farm.

Now, we have the tantric yoga session, which is going to test my willpower even further. I should've come up with some excuse when Romy originally brought it up.

The instructor comes to your home, and since my cottage is too small, we're back at Jude's. I'm on the porch, waiting for him to shower and change. I sip the white wine that he keeps chilled in the fridge for me and prop my feet up on the railing, wishing—as I do all the time lately—that our situation was different. I wish I was in this chair because we are a couple, and

I wasn't full of nerves about touching him in intimate ways today.

"What the hell do I wear?" Jude says, walking out the door in jeans and a T-shirt.

I look him up and down. "Not jeans."

"Shit. You know, I looked at some stuff online, and if you think I was a bad dancer, I'm going to royally suck at this." He walks back inside. "I'll be right back!"

I hear his footsteps pounding up the stairs before I hear a vehicle of some kind coming down the drive to his house. I down the rest of my wine, needing to get rid of any inhibitions about what's about to happen.

Romy parks the eight-seater limo-type UTV with The Knotted Barn logo on the hood at the end of the drive. The woman with her is dressed in a cute green sports bra and tight yoga pants. Her dark hair is pulled back into a high ponytail, and her face has a full-on makeup job.

I really should've upped my game. My oversized T-shirt over yoga pants isn't nearly as sexy as our instructor's outfit. Jude will be staring at her while I'm staring at him. He doesn't usually show other women attention when I'm around him, but every time I've caught him, it's been a brunette. This woman is Jude's type, and I want to run inside the house and lock her out.

"Better?" Jude says, walking out of the house and stopping, his gaze going to the woman's ass as she's bent over, grabbing her stuff from the back of the UTV.

Great. This is going to be fun.

"Hey, guys!" Romy waves, helping the woman with the mats.

When they walk up the porch steps, Jude hasn't said another word. Probably because he's distracted by the swell of the instructor's tits. I could never pull off a sports bra as a shirt since I barely have a handful.

"This is Autumn. She's your instructor for the day," Romy says.

Autumn smiles at us. "It's beautiful here. I've always wanted to live somewhere secluded like this."

Jude and I look at one another and laugh.

"My entire family lives on the ranch. Trust me, there's nothing secluded about it," Jude says.

Autumn's eyes roll over Jude as though he's going to star in her fantasies tonight. "Much more so than my small apartment in Lincoln. I might have to relocate here. Romy was just telling me that you might have an opening for a yoga instructor."

"Really?" Jude asks, eyeing Romy.

"Just something Scarlett and I have been throwing around. Nothing is for sure yet."

It's a weird dynamic at the ranch. It's all Noughton land, but Bruce took over the cattle farm years ago, since he was the only brother and the oldest sibling. His sisters, Jude's aunts Darla and Bette, both married and have since opened businesses of their own, which trickled down to Jude's six cousins finding ways to incorporate the things that interest them. But when it comes to doing anything on the family land, it has to be a group decision.

"We'll schedule a meeting," she says, which appeases Jude.

He takes the role of being the eldest cousin seriously, though Lottie always reminds him she's only three months younger.

"Hi, Autumn, I'm Sadie. The bride." I stand and put my hand between us.

"I love the early start." She eyes my wine glass on the table and situates her bags to shake my hand.

"And this is Jude, my cousin. The groom." Romy takes over the introductions, and I pick up my empty wine glass.

They shake hands a little too long for my liking.

"I can take your bags." Jude holds out his hands, and Autumn acts as if she's carrying fifty-pound weights, handing them over to Jude.

I really need to stop judging her. She's here to do a job, and Jude is a good-looking guy. Can I blame her for noticing?

"Okay, I'll leave you guys to it. Autumn, I'll swing by in two hours to pick you up." Romy steps down from the porch stairs.

"I'll drive her back," Jude says.

"Or I can," I offer. "On my way home."

Autumn laughs. "I think I'm covered. Thanks again, Romy."

"Seems like it. Thanks, guys." Romy walks to the UTV, starts it up, and drives off.

"Let's get started." I round Jude, since his hands are full, to open the door for her.

Autumn walks past me, and all I can think of is how many squats she has to do to get an ass like that.

She stops right inside the door, taking in the space. "What a lovely farmhouse. There are more modern touches than I would've assumed."

I slide by her. "Jude built the house himself."

Jude puts her bags on the floor by the door, the tips of his ears turning red from embarrassment. The man hates to be the center of attention.

"Seriously? Damn. You should do it for a living. It's beautiful."

He shrugs. "I'm a cattle rancher."

"Oh." Her smile falters a bit. "I guess everyone has to make a living."

If I'd known that would kill her attraction to him, I would've mentioned it sooner.

Jude helps her pair her phone to his Bluetooth speaker, and she goes over the definition of tantra and how our goal today is to grow the intimacy and sexuality between us. If she only knew the truth.

"Each of you grab a mat and put them right up against one another. Sit on your own. I'm going to put on some soothing background music."

She busies herself as we arrange the mats, my anxiety ramping up that we're going to be touching and staring into one another's eyes. I've watched videos online to prepare myself, hoping I can turn off my sexuality and do the poses without desire coursing through me the whole time.

"Please sit back to back, cross your legs, and relax your arms on your lap."

We do as she says, our spines aligned. Jude's muscled back feels so much stronger than my own.

"Now take deep breaths, in and out, feeling each other's energy."

Jude grunts, and I close my eyes, taking deep breaths, all too aware of Jude's presence so close to me. Every day, I struggle more and more to contain my feelings. I was so close to spilling all my feelings only weeks ago, and now I'm stuck in a stall pattern trying to save my family's farm, which got me here, in a private tantra yoga class with Jude's body pressed against mine.

I'm so lost in my thoughts that I spook when Autumn lifts my arm. "Now twist," she says softly, using a gentle tone as if she's afraid she's going to pull us out of the moment. "Your arm goes to this thigh."

She guides my hand to rest on Jude's right knee. His leg jolts but calms soon enough. She picks up his hand and puts it on my right knee, leaving our backs still touching but twisted more into one another.

Crap, this is a lot more intimate than I thought. In all the years we've been friends, Jude has probably never been this close to me for this long.

It feels nice though, hearing his breathing, feeling his back rise and fall. I do feel closer to him.

"You guys are perfect," she says. "Now come back to your starting position, but this time, Jude, you're going to lean forward, putting your elbows on the floor, and Sadie is going to move back, pressing her back to yours, stretching her core."

"Yeah, I don't bend like that," Jude says.

"Let's just try it. Surely riding a horse and lassoing innocent cows keeps you flexible."

I snicker, surprised that Jude isn't saying anything back. He's not usually one to keep his snarky comments to himself.

She pushes on his back, and he groans and grunts the entire time but does manage to bend into position. Autumn guides me by my hand, not telling me but showing me and putting me in the position she wants. I stretch my body over Jude's back, accepting and trusting that he has me as he always does.

"Lovely," she says. "You two are beautiful."

I'm sure she says that to all her couples. She's already mentioned her studio in Lincoln twice and a weekend retreat she's doing if we really want to connect. Kudos to Romy for bringing her in. Good for both of them on the business front.

"Now we're going to switch," she says.

"Good. I was getting a thigh cramp," Jude grumbles.

I shoot Autumn an apologetic look, but she doesn't seem to care.

"Sadie, you bend forward, and you're going to hold Jude's body on yours."

"I'll break her," he says.

"Trust me, she's a lot stronger than you think."

Huh. I think I'm actually starting to like Autumn.

Jude lies on my back, breathing in and out, and my mind betrays me, wondering if the weight of him on me feels similar to how it would if we were having sex and he was on top of me. How many times have I dreamed of that exact image?

"Perfect," Autumn says in a soothing voice.

I concentrate on the music, trying to push all the intrusive thoughts from my mind.

"Now, I want you two to face one another. This is the most intimate, but you guys will be naturals, I know it. Cross your legs and face one another, resting your arms on your legs, then stare into one another's eyes."

I look up from my lap, and Jude's gaze is on me. Our eyes lock, and Autumn sits on the floor by us as if she's our teacher and wants to make sure we don't cheat.

"Feel the love you have for one another. We're watering it with the hope it grows deeper roots. Make promises with your eyes."

She continues talking quietly, and it's not until she stops talking that tension builds around us.

"Slide closer, Jude. Be the giver, offering yourself to her."

He scoots closer, our knees touching. I swallow, lost in his brown eyes because there is love there, and for what feels like the millionth time, I wonder if I just spit out the truth of my feelings, how would he react?

"Rest your arms on each other's legs."

Jude's calloused palms land on my thighs and my stomach flutters. His muscled thighs flex under my hands and my fingers.

"I love you two. So easy." She presses her hand on my back. "Now, Sadie, you're going to straddle Jude."

"What?" Jude asks, whipping his head toward Autumn.

She chuckles. "I'm not asking you to whip it out and have sex. She's going to straddle you and wrap her legs around you. Then you'll hold her close."

I'm with Jude on this one.

"It's usually the groom's favorite part," Autumn says.

"Fine," he bites out.

Not exactly the invitation I was hoping for, but I get close, opening my legs to slide up on his lap. His eyes dip between my legs in the process of me getting on top of him.

"Just like that, Sadie. Now wrap your arms and legs around his body."

I position myself like a koala, and Jude is the tree.

"Jude, wrap your arms around her, hold her body tight and close."

He does, and I shift to get more comfortable, feeling something prominent at my core. Holy shit, he's got a hard-on.

"Stop shifting," he whispers.

Autumn stands and touches his shoulder. "Don't worry, it's a natural reaction."

"Jesus," he whispers.

"Stay like that until the music stops. Don't worry about little Jude wanting in on the action. Concentrate on one another. Little Jude will get his action after I leave." She laughs softly.

I close my eyes, but all the blood has traveled between my legs, and my core is pulsing. The feel of his hard length between my legs is all I can think about. Knowing I might never get to be this close to him again, I shamelessly grind into him, pretending to be trying to get more comfortable.

"Sadie..."

I shouldn't like the groan in his voice, but I do.

Whether Jude feels the same as I do for him, one thing is for sure, I turned him on tonight. The problem is that now I know exactly how big he is and that doesn't help douse the fire between my thighs.

Chapter Sixteen

JUDE

I couldn't be happier that the tantric yoga is over and Sadie agreed to drive Autumn back to her car at The Knotted Barn because I'm as embarrassed as the first time my dad found me beating off and decided to give me a talk about my body's mechanics. Yes, that's how he referred to it.

I'd discovered my dick felt good when I rubbed it. End of discussion.

After Sadie and Autumn drive away, I jog upstairs to relieve myself as if I'm that twelve-year-old boy again. Having Sadie's tits crushed to my chest and her pussy grinding against my dick made my hard-on painful.

I lie in my bed, grab my lube, and pull my shirt over my head, my shorts under my balls. I tug on my dick, not that he needs any warming up. The fucker is ready to explode with one thought of pulling Sadie's T-shirt over her head to feel the weight of her tits in my palms. She's not big-breasted, but they're enough for me to work with. I've had to painfully admire her nipples through her wet bikini too many times to not develop a clear image in my mind of those kissable buds.

I tighten my fist at the dream of touching her, running my

thumbs over her hard peaks, her tossing her head back from the exhilaration of having my hands on her. She bends at the waist, offering herself to me, and I rise up, taking a tit in my mouth, my teeth nibbling and teasing her as she grinds along my dick.

My hand increases speed, and I close my eyes, imagining flipping her over, tugging down those yoga pants, and finding her in a thong that shows me she's as turned on as I am. I trail kisses down her chest, my finger grazing under the elastic of her underwear and feeling how soaked she is—and all because of me.

"Fuck, Sadie," I murmur, my fist running up and down my length, my balls tightening. I'm gonna come before I even get us to the sex part.

In my mind, she's moaning, writhing under me, and I tug off her panties, shifting between her legs, throwing one leg over my shoulder, and running my nose along her swollen clit, smelling her for the first time. And she's just as sweet smelling as I thought she'd be.

My tongue laps at her slit, gliding up and down. Her body moves, her fists clenching my comforter. She's finally in my bed and allowing me to take her like I've wanted to for years.

She responds with moans each time I touch her, the knuckles of both of my hands running back up her body until my palms take her tits, pinching her nipples. Her back arches off the mattress, and she screams my name.

I'm unable to hold back any longer. Although I want to stay in my mind a little longer, my cum erupts out of my dick and warmth hits my stomach.

I let out a long exhale. Fuck, I needed that.

"Jude!" Sadie shouts, and I hear her footsteps on the stairs.

"Hold up," I call.

"I forgot we had to talk about songs."

I grab my T-shirt and wipe the cum off me right before she steps into my room, since the door is wide open.

"Oh god, I'm sorry." Her eyes land on my exposed, deflated dick.

Definitely not the impression I wanted to make the first time she ever saw it. Awesome.

I grab the elastic waist of my boxer briefs and tuck my dick back in.

"I shouldn't have come up! I'm sorry!" She covers her eyes a little too late.

"Open your eyes, Sadie," I say, getting off my bed.

"No!"

"I'm covered."

She peeks through her fingers and cringes. "I'm so sorry."

Her cheeks are the same color as the red lipstick she wears at Christmas when she wears her favorite holiday sweater. I go to my walk-in closet and dump the T-shirt in my hamper.

"It's fine." I'm trying to play it off, but I really hope she doesn't want to dissect this like my dad did all those years ago.

"I feel bad." She hasn't moved from the doorway when usually she would sit on my bed and wait for me to finish getting ready.

"Then I guess you have to show me your tits to keep things fair." I purposely don't laugh just to throw her off kilter, to change up the awkward energy in the room.

"Ha."

"I'm serious, Sadie. Have at it." I cross my arms and lean against the doorjamb of my closet, pretending to wait for her to unclothe.

"Shut up, Jude. We have to talk about songs."

She's so quick to change the subject that she must feel uncomfortable with the thought, but I love the flush that's now all over her body. If she thinks I missed her little grinds and shifting her weight over my dick during the tantric yoga session, she's sorely mistaken. She might not want me as a boyfriend or husband, but she needs some relief.

"Songs?" I walk toward the door, raising my hand to motion for her to go downstairs.

"We don't have a song to dance to at the wedding."

I nod. She walks down first, and my eyes go straight to her ass. How on earth am I going to marry this girl and move her into my house and *not* have sex with her? It's a feat made for a stronger man than me.

Once we're downstairs, she grabs her wineglass from earlier, filling it while I grab a beer. We head out to the porch, and she pulls out her phone, most likely connecting to my Bluetooth speaker.

"It wasn't that bad, right?" she asks, mindlessly looking at her phone.

"The yoga?"

One thing about Sadie is that if she doesn't want to discuss something, she has the ability to act as if it never happened. I guess we're playing the pretend-she-never-saw-my-dick game.

"Yeah. I was afraid she was going to have us do more stretches that I'd fail," she says.

"You'd fail? I thought my thighs were going to lock in place when she had me lean down with my forearms on the ground."

She laughs. "I don't think she cares for your line of business."

"I got that too."

"Okay." She straightens. "I looked up the most popular wedding songs. If we want to convince people we're a real couple, we need a song."

"To dance to?"

She sips her wine, tucking one leg under the other and facing me. I love how comfortable we are with one another.

One day, she's going to wise up and discover I can't give her what she wants and go looking for someone who can. "Yes. To dance to."

She plays the first song.

"Too fast," I say. "I did the dance lesson, but I'm not Fred Astaire."

"Fair enough. Next." She presses her thumb to the phone.

"Too slow."

She huffs but presses her thumb on the screen again. Another song starts.

"I've heard this at all ten weddings I've been to. Too common."

Her phone drops into her lap. "Okay, Mr. Hard To Please. Let's try this one." She presses the screen again.

"Too rock. I'd prefer country."

Her thumb presses harder on the screen, and she groans. Another song comes on.

"Too old-school country."

She tosses the phone into my lap, and my beer spills when I try to grab it. "Have at it, big guy."

Straightening in the chair, she stares at the water, watching those two ducks that haven't left yet.

"I'm sure I can find us one." There are a few that have always reminded me of Sadie, but I'm torn between two. "How about this one?"

I play "From the Ground Up" by Dan & Shay.

She sips her wine, and I listen to the words, my eyes unable to stray from her. The duo sings about building a life together, getting married and having a family. It's perfect for a wedding, and I'm sure it would bring tears to Sadie's mom's eyes. I always wanted to slow dance with her to this song when I imagined taking my shot and telling her my feelings.

"I like it," she says. "I think I saw it on a list."

I scroll through the music on her phone. "I have one more."

"Really? I thought it was perfect." There's a sheen of tears in her eyes.

I press play on "Your Everything" by Keith Urban.

The music plays, and she listens intently. I once again admire her sitting next to me. The lyrics speak about how much a man wants to be a woman's everything. To be the one who makes her smile and supports her in her dreams. And that's what I've always wanted to be to Sadie, but I doubt that I'm enough for her. I can't change the grumpy, quiet guy I am. She deserves someone like Ben, who isn't afraid to tell the whole world his feelings and show his affection.

God, she's so beautiful. She looks as though she's meant to be in that seat. I want the two of us sitting in this exact position, watching our kids play or enjoying early mornings before they wake or dark nights after they go to bed. It's a dream I've had many times, but I've never taken the chance on making it become a reality. I almost did once. But then things changed.

"I love it," she says, wiping tears from eyes. "It's perfect, Jude."

I nod. "Then it's done. We have a song. I need another beer."

I place her phone on the table between us and walk into the house. When I reach the kitchen, I rest my hands on the edge of the counter and take a moment to gather myself. To remind myself that she needs me right now. I can't make this about myself and my feelings.

I grab another beer and walk back out to the porch.

"So, when should I move in?" she asks when I sit down.

Fucking hell, I just got myself in check and now she's talking about moving in here.

I unscrew the cap of my beer and put it on the table. "Whenever you want."

"Oh, okay." She sounds upset.

I should reassure her. I didn't mean to be short, but that line between doing what's best for her and what my head and my heart—and apparently my dick—want is threadbare right now.

"I'll move you in after the wedding." I tip back my beer and gulp down half the damn bottle.

She doesn't say anything, and we both watch two ducks swim around the lake, ignoring everything we should be talking about. Things like how real this wedding is starting to feel and what it will mean for our future.

Chapter Seventeen

JUDE

The rehearsal went as well as could be expected. My boisterous family was rowdy and not listening to Romy's instructions at all. But when she pulled out a bullhorn and nearly made us all deaf, we fell into line.

We were going to have a cookout behind the house, but Gillian, the new woman in our family, said it's too cold, and when Emmett said we could do a bonfire, she shut that down too. So we're having a meal at The Knotted Barn. It's a buffet, and most people here are family and close friends.

Sadie's across the room in a dress that shows off her amazing legs. She's talking with her mom and my dad, and all three of them are laughing. I walk across the room to join their three-person circle.

"Jude." Dad nods, and Sadie and her mom part to allow me in. "I was just telling them about that time when Monty came to the house and said you were sneaking into Sadie's room."

Sadie puts her hand on my forearm. Her touch feels as normal as breathing at this point. "It was because Snowball died. Remember, I would cry at night because I was used to

143

him sleeping at the foot of my bed? So you'd climb up the terrace and sit with me until I fell asleep."

"You did?" Rhea looks at me with shock.

I'd forgotten about that.

"Monty thought you two were...well, he gave me this whole lecture about having a talk with my son about protection." My dad's face transforms into a smile that doesn't reach his eyes. "He'd be happy to see you two right now."

Rhea wipes a few tears from her eyes. "Yes, he would."

She gives me that look, which tells me she's thinking about the one secret I share with Rhea. The one I've never told Sadie. Not because it would hurt her—hell, it might even put her at ease tomorrow. But it would only complicate things at this point.

Sadie touches my dad's forearm. "Thank you for that story."

"I've got more whenever you want them." My dad smiles at her.

"I'll be right back." Sadie steps out of our circle, and I watch her disappear down the hallway toward the bathroom.

Lottie catches my eye and gives me a look that says Sadie's breakdown is coming soon.

"He really did always think you two would get together," Rhea says. "I know he gave you some hell over the years, but he knew how much you loved Sadie."

"I wish he could be here," I say.

"Amen to that." My dad takes a sip of his drink.

Rhea and I drink too.

"Excuse me," I say, walking away in the direction Sadie went, dropping my glass on a nearby table.

I lean against the wall outside the bathroom to wait for her. She comes out a few minutes later, dabbing her eyes. She looks up and startles.

"Jude." Her hand goes to her chest.

I hold out my hand to her. "Why don't we ditch this party?"

"It's our party."

"Exactly why it's okay. People will think we've snuck off to have a quickie or something."

She places her hand in mine, and I sneak us out the back door. We walk around the building and find the sun is just starting to set. My aunt Darla knew what she was doing when she had the barn erected here, overlooking the vineyard. It's the most romantic view I've ever seen. Perfect for a wedding venue.

"Where are we going?" Sadie asks, interrupting my thoughts.

The truth is, I just want to have some time with her before we separate before the wedding. I miss her. I miss the old us. Everything lately has been about the wedding, and I get why— we're throwing it together in two weeks—but I want to be with her away from everyone.

"I want to give you my wedding gift."

She stops and pulls her hand from mine. "I didn't get you a gift."

"I don't want a gift." I reach for her again, but she doesn't step forward. "Don't worry, it's not anything a usual groom would give his bride."

I drove us here after picking Sadie up from her house, so we climb into my truck and head toward the unused old barn on our cattle farm. She doesn't say much, her silence speaking more than words. Usually, she fills the space between us since I suck at conversation.

We pull up to the old barn, and I keep my headlights facing it since there aren't any working lights in there.

"Are we going to open those barn doors to some prized cow or something? I'm scared."

"No. Come on." I nod toward it, and she climbs out of the truck.

"Um, Jude…"

I round the front of the truck and see her heels are stuck in the mud.

"Do you have any boots in the truck?" she asks.

I bend down and put her over my shoulder. Her feet slip out of the shoes, and I pick them up, mud splattering on my slacks. But I don't care.

"Jude!" she yelps, but she doesn't fight as I walk to the barn.

"How else would you get there?" I open the barn doors and put her shoes on the wooden floor that's seen better days but will at least protect her heels from the mud. "Sorry about your shoes."

I lower her, and her body slides along mine as her feet slip back into her shoes. Our eyes lock for a moment, and as they've been doing lately, hers are filled with something different. Lust? Love? I'm not sure, but staring at Sadie feels different now somehow.

Her gaze strays first and she looks past me. "What's under the tarp? A new truck? I told you, I love my Datsun. It makes me feel closer to my grandma."

"It's not a new truck." I walk over and take the edge of the tarp in hand. "It's so much better. At least, I think so."

I tear off the tarp, revealing the mobile free-range chicken coop I've been working on the past couple weeks based on some research I did. Sadie doesn't say a word. She doesn't scream or jump up and down. Her hands cover her mouth, and she stares at it.

I shift in place. "I followed what I saw online but made some tweaks. I put it on wheels so we can move it around the acreage and let them feed in different spots. We can add—"

"It's beautiful." Her gaze flicks over to me. "This is the

best wedding gift." Sadie walks closer to get a better look and touches every part she comes to.

"We can duplicate it. It didn't take me long to make it."

A tear slips down her cheek, and she wipes it away, but another one comes right after, then another. Her back shakes as she cries openly while she walks around the chicken coop, inspecting every inch.

It feels as if someone has cracked open my chest. "Did you want to do it together? Did I overstep?"

She shakes her head, walking toward me as her eyes remain on the chicken coop.

"No. It's so..." Her head falls into her hands, and she cries even harder.

"Sadie," I whisper, wrapping my arms around her.

She slides her arms around my waist in a tight grip, inching up on her tiptoes and burying her face in my neck.

I run my hands over her back. "What's wrong? I thought you'd be happy."

She nods. "I am," she croaks, her grip only growing tighter.

"Then what is it?" Panic constricts my breathing, a million thoughts racing through my head—what's going on, what can I do to fix it, can I fix it?

Her heels fall to the floor, and she unwinds her arms. She wipes her tears with the backs of her hands. "It's everything. This." She points at the chicken coop. "I can't imagine doing this with anyone else, but I didn't think that my dad wouldn't be here for my wedding. That I'd have to ask my mom to walk me down the aisle. He's going to miss everything. He won't ever meet his grandkids, and that's if I ever truly get married."

She sits on a bench, and the tears topple over one another down her cheeks. This is what Lottie's warning was about. It's the night before our wedding, and she's falling apart.

"Not that it matters, right? We're not marrying for love.

We're not going to have kids. After I secure the loan and get the land in black, I'll probably be too old to have kids. So maybe he's not missing out on anything anyway."

I try to catch up to her thoughts, unsure which direction I should go to try to make her feel better.

"I'm just so scared. Scared I can't do what it takes to make this business successful. Scared I can't save my family farm. Scared I'm going to ruin your future, and you'll lose your land. Scared about—" She stops speaking abruptly. "Just everything."

"What else? Get it out. You'll feel better." I squat in front of her, wiping the tears from her red-rimmed eyes.

"Scared that I'll lose you with all this. I mean." Her hand raises in the direction of the chicken coop again. "Look how much you did for me."

I shake my head emphatically. "You'll never lose me. No matter what happens in the future, I'm always gonna be here for you. Always." And I mean every word.

I'm more afraid she's going to find someone else and move on. If I really dig deep into why I was so willing to do this fake marriage thing, it's probably some fucked up selfish need to lock her down a little longer, not give her a chance to meet someone. She shouldn't be worried about losing me. I could be destroying her chance to have kids just because I'm a selfish bastard.

She gives me a soft smile. "Tomorrow, we have to kiss." Her shoulders fall a bit.

It takes me a second to keep up with her ping-ponging thoughts. "I know."

"I don't want my first kiss with you to be in front of everyone."

I rise to my feet and sit on the bench next to her. "What do you mean?"

"What if it's weird when we kiss, and we aren't convincing?"

"It's just a kiss." I shrug.

I've had the same worry but for different reasons. What if the kiss is too intense, and I can't stop? Or what if there isn't any chemistry there, and all this tension has nowhere to go?

"Yeah, but we're supposed to be in love."

I bring my hand up to her face and turn her my way. "I can't squash all your fears, but I can take one away." I bring my mouth to hers.

"I'm not sure—"

"It's too late," I whisper, my lips millimeters from hers. She turns her head, offering me her cheek, and I trail my lips along her cheek toward her ear. "Do you want me to stop?"

She fists my shirt and slides closer to me on the bench. "No."

I turn her face with my hand on the back of her neck, bringing our lips so close I smell her sweet wine breath. I place my lips on her soft plump ones, and it's incredible. She's incredible.

Sadie releases my shirt, and I wrap my free hand around her waist, tugging her up and onto my lap, kind of like we did for tantric yoga. Her fingers play with my hair as I devour her mouth, and she settles her weight on me. Our tongues explore, gliding and learning the taste of each other.

Fuck. This was my worst idea ever.

She grinds her hips, and I want to take this so much further. I want to strip this dress off her and lay her down on the bench, slide my hand between her legs and find out how wet she is. I want her to unbuckle my pants and pull out my dick so I can run it along her damp panties. After years of what I thought was enough beat-off material, with one kiss, Sadie gives me another decade's worth.

She strips her lips off mine, and I inch forward, not wanting to stop, the picture of a desperate man.

"Oh god." She touches her swollen lips with her fingers and stares at me in awe.

"Sadie..."

She quickly climbs off my lap, straightening her dress. "So, I guess we're good there, huh?"

"Yeah." I stand and adjust myself.

Her eyes dip to my movement, and she steps forward. For a moment, I think she's going to kiss me again. I'd snatch her up so fast, she'd have no time to react before my lips were on hers.

But she stops. "We should get back."

"Yeah, right." I grip the back of my neck.

She walks out of the barn, and her calves flex as she tries not to get her heels stuck in the mud. I watch her climb into the truck, then I shut the barn and join her.

"Thank you," she murmurs.

She's thanking *me*? She's blind to the fact that she just made my fucking year. But it's easy to see she's not ready for anything between us.

With all the chaos, I momentarily forgot that she's got a lot on her plate. She's still grieving, and the pressure to save her family's farm is at the forefront of her mind, rightfully so. The last thing she needs is for me to throw all my bullshit her way, so I keep my mouth shut and drive us back to the rehearsal dinner.

Chapter Eighteen

SADIE

L ottie knocks and peeks her head into the room. "How's the bride?"

I stare at the dress I bought online, hanging on the closet door in the bridal suite of The Knotted Barn. It's a pretty dress, but I didn't get to go to a bridal shop to find it. Nothing today is what I thought my wedding day would entail. Tears fill my eyes.

"Oh, Sadie." Lottie comes into the room, shutting and locking the door. "Don't cry."

I blot my eyes since I already did my makeup. "I'm fine. It's just..."

She sits beside me on the couch, and her hand falls to my knee. "I know. This isn't your dream."

I shake my head, afraid to talk in case more tears slip free. I was holding it all together until last night.

"You have to think about what could happen from this. It might end up being the best thing for the two of you."

"I think I'm making a mistake." I inhale a big breath and go to sit at the vanity to do my hair.

"Then call it off. I'll go out there and tell everyone you don't want to marry Jude."

I stare at her reflection in the mirror. "Then you'd be a liar."

She gives me that expression to say she's sorry, which she doesn't have to be. She's not any part of this. "I know you want to save the farm, but is this worth it?"

She takes the curling iron from my hand and separates my hair to curl.

"It is. For my mom and the memory of my dad. I just needed to grieve what I'll never get."

"Sadie. You will." Our eyes lock in the mirror. "You will get your dream wedding someday. Sadly, it might not be with Jude, but I'll be damned if you don't get it."

"And how do you think I'll meet this mystery man when I'm married to Jude?"

She smiles, and her head bobs right and left. "That's a good question, but this marriage isn't forever, right? The more successful the farm is, the sooner you're out of it."

Isn't that the problem? I don't want out of this marriage. I just wish it was real.

"We've never talked about how long we'll stay married. Probably something we should have discussed." I frown.

Lottie curls my hair into perfect ringlets, and my nerves calm a little. This is Jude I'm marrying. So what if I don't have the big wedding I always dreamed of? I'm technically marrying the man of my dreams.

"You know what? Who cares? This is just a formality. It's not the wedding day that matters. It's the fact I'm marrying Jude. And maybe it's not for love, but he's doing me a big favor, and I appreciate it so much. I don't have anything to complain about."

She puts down the curling iron and places her hands on my shoulders. "Sadie, it's okay to want more. You can tell me. I know it won't change the fact that you're going to walk down that aisle to Jude, but I'm here to talk about whatever you want. No judgment."

She picks up the curling iron again, and I concentrate on her sliding a chunk of my hair into the curling iron and twisting it around.

"What I want isn't available to me. Maybe something will come from this." Not that I'm allowing my mind to go there, because I'd be setting myself up for disappointment.

"I'm sure if you strut around his house naked, it'll do the trick. Men are easy creatures." She puts down the curling iron and grabs the hair spray.

"Are you speaking from experience?" When she gives me a confused look, I say, "Brooks?"

She rolls her eyes and sprays my hair. "We're not talking about me today."

Lottie says she hates Brooks, and maybe she does, but I wouldn't make coffee before my store opens for a man I hate. Maybe she likes the attention he gives her. She's always so closed off when I try to talk about him.

"You are aware that his gaze is always on you," I say. "I mean, he took a baseball to his junk this summer because you distracted him with your amazing ass."

She shakes her head. "Brooks only wants what he can't have."

"I'm not sure—"

"Let's just not talk about Brooks." She finger-combs my curls, and they turn out just as I wanted. They wouldn't have looked as beautiful if I'd done them myself.

"Thank you, my hair looks perfect."

"It only looks good because you're gorgeous. Let's get you in your dress." She slips the dress off the hanger. "It's a beautiful dress, Sadie."

"It is...I think I just always had this dream of trying on

153

gowns with you and my mom and whoever else. But I do love this one."

I tried it on a few days ago in my cottage in front of my long mirror, and the fit was perfect.

I take off my robe and step into the dress. The top is lace with more of a dip than I thought I'd like, and the skirt doesn't poof out, but there are layers, and it's loosely pleated, falling down my legs.

After Lottie zips me up, a knock sounds on the door. Lottie goes over to open it.

"Delivery," Ben says and winks at me, handing Lottie a note and a bouquet of flowers wrapped in paper.

"He got her flowers?" Lottie asks skeptically, since it's not very Jude-like.

"Sure did. I'm rubbing off on him. See you in a bit."

Ben disappears down the hall, and Lottie comes over, handing me the flowers. "Figures Jude doesn't do roses."

No, he didn't. He did something so much better, and all those nerves that told me to seek him out in the groom's room to shut down this marriage of convenience dissipate.

"They're wildflowers," I whisper.

"Exactly."

I shake my head, tears welling in my eyes again. "I used to pick wildflowers for my bouquet when I made Emmett marry me."

She laughs. "I forgot about that. I just remember that ratty old white dress your mom bought you at the second-hand store that you wore for an entire year."

I smile at the flowers. "It wasn't a year."

"Are you sure?" She uses the hairspray in her hair, staring in the mirror. "Want some privacy to read the letter?"

"Would you mind?" I pick up the envelope with my name scribbled across the front in Jude's messy handwriting.

"Not at all. I'll be outside when you're ready."

I grab the letter and slide my finger along the seam. It's a short note, scribbled in the same handwriting as the envelope.

Sadie,

Sadly for you, you're getting me today instead of Emmett.

There are a lot of emotions today, and I'm sure you're second-guessing what we're doing. But I hope this note will calm you. It's me, Jude, your best friend, you're marrying today. I hope I've been there for you as many times as you have been for me. What we're embarking on is scary, but it's us. Me and you. We've got this. There's no reason to be scared because I'll always catch you. Never doubt that. Always.

Yours,
Jude

I fold up the letter and tuck it back in the envelope, then slide it into my purse so no one else finds it. He's right. It's us, and we've gotten through a lot over the years. He's always been there to pick me up when I fall, and I've done the same for him. I have nothing to fear.

I step out of the hallway and find Lottie talking to my mom.

"Lottie said you needed some time alone." My mom steps up to me, her hand cradling my cheek. "You make a beautiful bride."

"Thank you, Mom. Ready to give me away?"

She nods, and tears pool in her eyes. "I'm sorry, It's just... your dad."

"I know." I swallow hard past the lump in my throat.

Lottie gently squeezes my shoulder. "I'll meet you two at the doors."

"He would have asked you one last time, so I'm going to as well. Don't get angry, but are you sure you want to do this?"

I give her a warm smile. "Yes, Mom, I'm positive."

She nods. "Good enough for me. Let's go get you married."

I circle my arm through hers, and she pats my hand, walking me to the doors that will open to our ceremony. I'm happy to be getting married here, overlooking the vineyard.

"Ready?" Lottie asks, nodding to her brother, Bennett, to open the doors.

His daughter Wren walks out first in her flower girl dress, dropping petals down the white runner toward the barn doors where our officiant and Jude will be standing since the weather is nice. Mother Nature is on our side today and gave us a glorious early fall day, the sun peering down on us.

Lottie walks after Wren, and once she's at the end of the aisle, my mom and I step up, waiting for the wedding march.

"Your father gave Jude your hand three years ago," my mom whispers. "And I know he's here today, smiling down on you from heaven. I just know it."

Her words take a moment to sink in. "What?"

"Your dad. His spirit is here." She smiles at me.

"No, before that. Three years ago?"

She shakes her head. "I shouldn't have said anything."

"What do you mean Dad gave him my hand three years ago?"

The wedding music starts, and I hear people standing and turning back to watch me walk down the aisle.

"Well…" Her expression suggests she's kept something from me, that she has a secret.

The music stops and starts again.

"We can talk about it later." Mom pats my hand. "It's time."

I turn to face everyone, and all their eyes are on me. Jude stands at the end of the aisle, his hands at his side and no smile. Does he not want to marry me? Or is it just his nerves?

I step forward, my mom urging me to go. For once, she's walking faster than I want. The whole time I make my way across the white runner toward Jude, my mind spins to remember what might have happened three years ago and what my mom could possibly be talking about.

We stop at the end. There's no veil for my mom to lift, so she kisses my cheek and squeezes my hand, lifting it and offering it to Jude. He smiles at her and helps me to stand next to him, the two of us facing one another on the terrace under the sun while all of our guests are seated inside the barn.

This is my dream. I'm marrying Jude Noughton. Concentrate on that, I tell myself.

"We're gathered here today to witness Sadie Wilkins and Jude Noughton…" the officiant starts.

Three years ago, Jude fell off Titan and was hospitalized for a concussion. But what does that have to do with my dad offering my hand in marriage to him?

Chapter Nineteen

SADIE

"I'm exhausted." I walk into Jude's house and slip off my heels, wanting out of this dress.

The ceremony and the reception went off without a hitch, and no one suspected anything other than we were happy.

Jude unbuttons the top two buttons on his shirt and untucks it from his pants, sitting down next to me, putting his feet up on the coffee table. "Me too."

Although I enjoyed pretending to be Jude's bride, my mom's words before I walked down the aisle stayed on my mind for most of the night.

"Hey," I say, tucking my legs under my body and facing him.

His head is leaned back on the sofa, and his eyes are closed. "Hmm?"

"My mom said something to me right before I walked down the aisle."

"'Kay?"

"She said three years ago, my dad gave you my hand in marriage."

His eyes open slowly, but he doesn't look at me.

"Do you know anything about that?"

Turning his head to face me, his expression says that he knows exactly what my mom meant. "It's nothing."

"Jude..."

He turns his gaze back to the ceiling. "Let's just go to bed."

"Neither of us is going to bed until you tell me the secret you've been keeping from me."

He groans and stands, heading into the kitchen. After grabbing water from the fridge, he stays in there, leaning over his island counter. "It's nothing to be concerned about."

I meet him in the kitchen and sit on one of the stools. "That's for me to decide."

He tips back the water bottle and finishes almost half of it.

When he doesn't say anything, I sigh. "Okay, I'll start. Three years ago, you fell off Titan, right?"

His fingers twist the cap back onto the bottle. "I did."

"And..." This is one thing about Jude. I have to pull information and emotions out of him.

"And I was in the hospital."

I throw my hands in the air. "Seriously, just tell me."

He leaves the kitchen, walking past the island. "You don't need to know. Go to bed, Sadie."

I hear his footsteps go up the stairs. We decided I'd spend the night in the spare room to keep up appearances that we're in love with one another. His bedroom door shuts a few seconds later.

If he thinks I'm not getting this information now after he's being so cagey, he's delusional.

I lift the hem of my dress, following him up the stairs. I don't bother knocking. Instead, I open the door of his bedroom.

"Fuck, Sadie." He already has his shirt unbuttoned,

showing the six-pack I already knew was hidden underneath. His hands move to his pants, buttoning them back up.

"Tell me," I say, crossing my arms.

"I'm not going to tell you. Go to bed."

"Are you going to tell me in the morning?"

"Probably not." He walks into the bathroom, pulls out his toothbrush, and puts toothpaste on it.

I steal the brush out of his hand and sit on the counter in front of him to block his nighttime routine.

He pinches the bridge of his nose. "You're not gonna let this go, are you?"

"No."

He steps back, running his hand through his hair and sitting on the edge of his Jacuzzi tub. "Falling off Titan fucked me up. Made me think...realize...that life is short. Probably my mom dying so young on the farm had something to do with it too, but I just..." He grips the back of his neck and looks at the floor between his feet.

I remain silent since he's finally giving me information.

"I went to your dad and told him I wanted to date you. Told him my intentions and that although I wasn't going to ask you to marry me right away, I wanted him to know how much you meant to me. That I wouldn't just start dating you on a whim, it was serious for me."

My entire body goes numb, and I rest my back against the mirror, needing something to support me. He had feelings for me? "Really?"

His eyes rise to meet mine. "Yeah." Jude clears his throat. "Your dad told me that I had your hand whenever I wanted it. That he always knew we'd end up together and knew I'd take care of you."

My nose burns, and my eyes fill with tears. "Why would you keep this from me? All this time..." I slide off the counter and walk into his bedroom. "You know how much peace that would have offered me today?"

He follows me. "Sadie, I—"

I whip around. "What, Jude?"

He doesn't say anything, refusing to finish the sentence.

I'm so mentally drained after the wedding today, the absence of my father, and now this. My parents and Jude. Three of the most important people in my life kept this from me all these years.

"What, Jude?" I say louder than I usually am.

"Then you were offered that job in New York, and I couldn't take that opportunity away from you." He sits on the edge of the bed, resting his forearms on his thighs, and puts his head in his hands.

I sit next to him and stare at him. "You should have told me."

He presses his thumbs into the bridge of his nose and stares at the floor. "It was your chance to get out of Willow-brook. To go fulfill your dreams."

Three years ago, I was approaching thirty. I'd gotten restless and applied for some jobs around the country, unsure if I really stood a chance of getting one of them. But I was offered a job by a company interested in my graphic design ability, and I accepted. I moved to New York because my grandma said she'd take care of my mom. Then my grandma died unexpectedly two months later, and I returned home. I always felt that was a saving grace though. I had been so homesick in New York, but too proud to return on my own.

"So, you had feelings for me?" I ask, nervous for his answer even though he's already confirmed that he did. "I mean, more than friends?"

His head falls down, his chin hitting his chest. "Do we really have to do this?"

"Yes."

He stays in place for a second then straightens. "Fine." Standing, he puts his hands in his pockets and steps away from me. "After the incident with Titan, I realized I'd been wasting so much time not taking my chances with you. I had plans to tell you everything I felt for you. But I wanted it to be perfect, so I waited a couple days. By the time I had it all planned, you'd gotten that job offer. I made your parents promise not to tell you about my conversation with your dad. I didn't want my feelings to have any bearing on whether you decided to take the job or not. So when you decided to move to New York, I didn't say anything so you could go and live out your dream."

Exhilaration wars with anger in my chest. I'm unsure how to react. We lost that time together...

"And now?" I whisper, swallowing my nerves.

He looks at me. "Now what?"

"How do you feel now?" I hold my breath, waiting for his answer.

He leans his back against the wall and stuffs his hands into his pockets. "Nothing's changed."

"Meaning?"

"Are you asking if I still have feelings for you?"

I stand and step closer to him. "I'm asking if you have feelings stronger than friendship for me."

Jude nods, his eyes swimming with love.

"Were you ever going to tell me?" I whisper.

He shakes his head. "No."

"But I came back. Why didn't you tell me then?"

I reach for him, but he walks across the room, dodging me. "Things came up."

"Bullshit."

He looks over his shoulder at me. "I'm not..."

"What?"

"I'm not one of those guys."

"What kind of guy?"

"I'm not Ben." His arms fly out at his sides.

"I don't remember ever asking you to be Ben."

He strips off his shirt and tosses it on the chair in the corner. "I really want this conversation to be over."

"Then tell me," I say, continuing to push him out of his comfort zone. We've come so far. I'm not backing down now.

"What do you want to know, Sadie?" His voice rises. "That I fucking love you, but I can't tell you? That I've wanted you most of my life, knowing you deserve someone who isn't...me?"

Tears block my vision for a moment before I blink, and they fall down my cheeks. "You love me?"

"Isn't it obvious?"

I shake my head. "No, it's not. Not at all."

He groans and pushes both hands through his hair, letting his head rock back to stare at the ceiling. "It's embarrassing. Can you please just leave and go to bed and forget all this shit?"

I step close to him. "You're an idiot."

He pushes his hands in his pockets and stares at me. "I'm aware."

I shake my head. "No, we're both idiots. God, Jude...I've loved you for as long as I can remember. And all this time..."

"What?"

My fingers crawl over his abs, up his chest, to rest around his neck. "I love you too," I whisper through tears.

"You do?"

I laugh. "I do."

His hands slide out of his pockets, and he winds them around my waist. "Sadie, it doesn't change the fact—"

I put my finger on his lips to stop his doubts from filling every inch of this room. "No. You, Jude. You are the man I want. I know all your faults and all your amazing qualities as well. I don't care that you're not like Ben. I love you exactly how you are."

He tugs me closer. "Fuck, Sadie." He rests his forehead against mine.

It might take him longer than me to believe my words, but he'll believe he's the right man for me. I'm going to make sure.

"Where do we go from here?" he asks.

"Well, I haven't gotten last night's kiss out of my mind." We shared some chaste kisses at the ceremony and the reception, but nothing like last night. "How about we start with another kiss?"

He holds my gaze, looming over me, and I inch up, our lips meeting. He's sweet and tentative, not rushing. His thumbs rub circles over my hips, his fingers tightening as if he's restraining himself.

God, I can't wait to have him. A euphoric sensation hits me, and my tongue slides over his lips. He chuckles but opens for me, his hands gliding to my ass.

He tastes like the red velvet cake from after dinner, and our kiss turns more frantic. Jude runs one hand up my back, sliding it into my hair and angling my head, exploring my mouth with his tongue. My core clenches, wanting more.

Just when I can't get enough of the kiss, he strips his lips off me, trailing them down my neck.

"Is this real?"

"Very much." His teeth nip at my collarbone. "Can I take off your dress?"

"Please," I beg.

His fingers search for and find the zipper, the sound filling every corner of the room. I'm about to be naked in front of Jude. Oh god, my best friend is about to see all of me.

I step out of his hold, and he falls forward but catches himself.

"Did I overstep?"

I shake my head. "I...I suddenly got nervous."

"We don't have to. We can wait. Whatever you want."

"No. I don't want to."

"Okay. That's fine. Your decision."

I chuckle. "I don't want to *wait*." I place one hand on the sleeve of my dress and slip it off my shoulder. Then I do the same with the other side. I push my dress so it puddles to the floor.

Jude's eyes flare with lust. "You're stunning."

"Are you just going to stand there?" I ask, smiling at him, calming my nerves because it's Jude. I have nothing to worry about.

"So, it's a yes?" he asks.

"Yes."

He rushes at me and takes me in his arms. "Thank fuck."

His lips land on mine again. This time, I'm not letting anything get in the way of having the wedding night I always dreamed of with Jude Noughton.

Chapter Twenty

SADIE

My core presses along his length. The same hardened length I couldn't stop grinding against last night in the barn. A moan slips from my mouth, and my hands fall to the waist of his slacks.

He looked so handsome tonight in his traditional tuxedo and cowboy boots, it was hard to tear my gaze away from him.

Giving me room, he steps back so I can unfasten his pants. My fingers graze his skin, and his stomach sucks in, his breath hitching. I lower his zipper, and my fingers slide to his hips, pushing the pants down until they rest at his ankles. His hands hold my face, cradling my cheeks, and I look at him. My heart beats too fast, too hard for this man. How did I ever last this long without having him like this?

Jude's an easy man to admire in his black boxer briefs, his muscular thighs on display. Farm work has done his body good over the years.

He must grow impatient because he crushes his lips to mine, his tongue seeking entrance, which I happily offer him. My knuckles trace down his sides, and I cup his length through the thin fabric. I rub my hand up and down the bulge. He pulls away from our kiss, his forehead resting on mine.

Taking the sides of his boxer briefs, I tug them down his legs, falling to my knees in front of him. His dick is impressive. I knew it would be. I fist the base, my mouth inching forward, but Jude stops me with his hand on my cheek.

"Later. I need you. I've waited a lifetime, and I want to be inside you."

Offering me his hand, I accept, and he raises me off the floor. I'm just as eager for him to be inside me. But I do want to be the one sucking him off when he comes so hard he yells. I want to be the one to bring him past the point of being able to control his reaction.

He makes quick work of my strapless bra and white lace panties. This is the last thing I thought would happen tonight, but I wanted to feel beautiful all in white.

Taking my hand, he leads me to the bed and sits me down on the edge. "Do you have any idea how beautiful you are?"

"I don't mind you reminding me." I give him a cheeky smile. and he chuckles.

He urges me up on the bed, his knee sinking down on the mattress, crawling after me. On his way up to my mouth, he stops at my breasts, sucking on one, and I feel like a star shooting through the galaxy. His tongue twirls around my nipple and moves to the other one, doing the same thing before he plants small kisses up to my mouth, settling his hips between my thighs.

The tip of his dick sits snug at my opening, but he doesn't slide in. Instead, he gets up on his knees, gripping his cock, pumping up and down. My eyes fixate on his movements, my mouth salivating, wishing I was feeling him pulsating in my palm.

"You still have that IUD?" He inches forward, running the tip over my clit and down my slit, over and over, my wetness coating him while my breath grows labored. "Fuck, you're wet."

"Yeah."

Jude knows everything about me. I complained to him at the time about how painful the insertion was.

He falls on his forearms, hovering over me as if he's worried about crushing me, but I love the feel of his weight over me. He kisses my cheek, then the corner of my lips until he sinks inch by slow inch inside me.

Our gazes lock and hold, his eyes overflowing with love, and I feel as though my chest might explode, it feels so full of joy right now. He slips out and back in, working himself deeper with every slide. We both moan. He inches out and thrusts back in. His pelvic bone hits my clit, and I gasp.

"Again," I pant.

He withdraws, and I miss the feel of him inside me, but he grinds back to the hilt, and heat spreads across my skin. I widen my legs, giving him the space he needs, and he accepts it, his hips pistoning back and forth.

Needing friction on my clit, I wrap my legs around his waist, and his thrusts increase in pace. I grip his shoulders, my fingertips needing to grab on to something because my core is vibrating, begging for a release, but I clench, not wanting this moment to end.

Thrust after thrust, he watches me, our eyes catching as often as our breaths. We've both waited so long for this moment, and I'm already looking forward to the next time. He angles his hips, and his pelvic bone rubs along my clit, the swollen bud greedy with want and need.

"Jude, I'm going to..."

"Come. Yes. I can't wait to see you come."

He thrusts in and out of me faster and deeper until my orgasm breaks past all my barriers. I close my eyes, my vision filling with stars as I cry out his name.

"Oh god." My body jolts forward, a warmth consuming my body.

He doesn't stop moving inside me. He crashes his lips to mine, his tongue desperate and needy. Just as quickly, he tears them from me, pumping into me, stilling, then his dick twitches inside me.

"Sadie," he groans in my ear, sucking the lobe into his hot mouth.

I'm back to wanting him more than before we started.

He collapses on me, and I wrap my arms around his torso, loving the feeling of flesh against flesh. I sigh and sink into the mattress.

"That was..." he says.

"Perfect," I finish for him.

He rises up on his forearms. "I love you, Sadie."

The confidence with which he says the words takes me aback. Could I have opened Jude Noughton's vault? God, I hope so.

I run my hands over his damp hair. "And I love you."

His smile could light up the New York skyline.

"How about a shower?"

"As long as you wash me," I say with a grin.

He slips out of me and offers me his hand. "You won't be lifting a finger."

I accept his hand, and we walk into the bathroom. All my dreams are coming true, and I'm not sure how to process how we got here. But I'm also not going to question it because it's all I've ever wanted.

Jude turns on the shower, putting his hand under the stream to make sure the water is warm enough. I slide into the small room that houses the toilet to pee and clean myself up.

When I come out, he's got two plush towels on the counter, and he's holding my brand of shampoo and conditioner. "You forgot them that time you stayed the weekend because the cottage was being exterminated."

I wrap my arms around his neck while he slides his arms around me. He kisses my forehead.

"You worried me for a second," I say.

"That I was some creep who bought your shampoo and beat off with it?" He chuckles.

I lightly smack his chest. "Ew. No, I thought they were another woman's."

"So, you're saying I shouldn't use your shampoo as lube?" His chest vibrates on my cheek.

"Can we stop now?"

"Maybe I wash my pubic hair with it? Guess you'll find out when you go down on me."

"Okay." I slide out of his arms, but he tugs me back to him.

"You think you're getting away now? Not a chance."

I place my hand on his chest and kiss him on the cheek. "I'm cold."

He opens his shower door for me, and I duck under his arm, stepping into the steam-filled space. He follows and shuts the door, allowing me to stand under the stream of water. The warmth feels so good on my skin, but it's nowhere near the same as when Jude's hands are on me.

He urges me to tip my head back, running his hand down my hair. "Turn around," he says, his hands directing my hips.

With my back to him, I hear the squirt of the shampoo bottle, then his fingers are threading through my hair. He lathers my scalp, and I moan, tipping my head farther back, needy for more.

"I wish you would've told me when I came home from New York." Now that I'm not in an orgasm haze, my mind can't stop playing the what-if game. What if my mom hadn't slipped? What if he'd said something sooner? Where would we be now if he'd told me back then? Would we already have kids of our own?

"You had your grandma's passing and your mom's health to deal with. I was scared. Hell, I'd be lying if I told you I'm not still scared." His hands fall to my hips, and he circles me back so my hair is under the water. "Time to rinse."

"Scared of what?"

He doesn't answer, concentrating on getting the shampoo out of my hair.

"Jude?"

"Do you remember when my mom died?"

How could I ever forget? It was a dark cloud over the entire town. My mom cried all the time.

"Yeah."

"Do you remember coming to the cemetery...when I cried?"

"That's when you started being nicer to me."

He pulls me to him, his dick hitting me in the stomach. "Nice to you?"

"Before your mom died, you treated me like I was a pain to be around. Always telling me I had to be the cheerleader and couldn't play football. But after your mom died, you'd pick me for your team sometimes."

He laughs. "I don't remember any of that. Shit, I'm sorry." He kisses my lips briefly then twirls his finger.

I turn my back to him when I'd rather be looking at him. The squirt of conditioner sounds before his hands run down my strands again.

"Anyway, you never told anyone I cried."

"I told you I wouldn't." And I never would.

"Well, after that, I didn't want to lose you. In a weird way, I got you after Mom died, and I thought that if you didn't feel the same or if you did, and I fucked it up...that scared me. The more weeks that went by, the more I lost my nerve, and I wasn't willing to risk it because I'm not sure I can survive without you in my life."

"Jude." I circle back, and his hands slip from my hair. "You'll never lose me. I promise you right now. No matter what happens, I'll always be in your life."

He moves me under the water and threads his fingers through my wet hair, tilting my head to rinse the conditioner.

"Do you believe me?" I stare at him, but he won't look at me.

"Time for soap."

I push at his chest until I'm out of the stream of water. "Talk to me."

He runs his palm along my cheek and rubs his thumb over my bottom lip. "It will just take time. That's all. I think I've done enough talking tonight."

He grabs the washcloth he brought in with him and squirts soap on it, lathering it under the water.

"I'm going to prove it to you. Just so you know."

He runs the washcloth over me, and my core clenches and aches to have him again.

"You never have to prove anything to me." He kisses my shoulder before inching me under the water.

Once I'm all clean, I slide along his body to get him under the spray, but his hands on my hips stop me, and he pushes me against the wall. His lips smash to mine, his hard dick pushing against my stomach while our slick bodies slide together. He hitches my leg over one of his hips, and I hold myself steady with my arms around his neck while he sinks into me.

I let him distract me with sex. Maybe he's only given me one number to the vault code, but when I'm done with him, I'll crack it open even if I have to take a sledgehammer to it. I'm going to free Jude Noughton of his demons.

Chapter Twenty-One

JUDE

We have two things on our agenda today. One is to secure the loan, and the second one is to grab all of Sadie's stuff and move her into my house. She's close enough that if anything should happen to her mom, she can race over there, and she can still take her mom to her appointments. Plus, she'll still be working out of the cottage when she's doing her graphic design work.

I park the truck in front of the bank. Sadie's hand goes to the door handle, and I stop her with my hand on her free one.

She turns around. "What?"

"I get your door now."

She smiles and her hand falls to her lap. "Oh, okay."

I grab the keys and climb out, going around the front of the truck to her door. I open it and offer her my hand. She slides her smooth, small hand into my calloused one, stepping down onto the running board then onto the ground next to me.

"Thanks."

"You don't have to thank me. It's my job." I keep my hand in hers, entwining our fingers, and lead us over to the bank.

"I never would have thought you'd be such a gentleman."

I grab the door handle but don't open it. "You thought I'd be some slug? I've been opening doors for you all of my life. You weren't even my girlfriend."

"True, but you wanted me to be your girlfriend." She bats her eyelashes.

"That does remind me, I think your coming out party is tonight."

"Coming out?" she asks, a wrinkle forming at the bridge of her nose.

I open the door and step inside. "How long you wanted me but didn't say anything." I raise my eyebrows, and she laughs.

"Every woman has her secrets."

"This isn't one of them."

"Sadie!" Cora waves. She went to high school with us, and I've always found her slightly annoying. Mostly because she used to tease Sadie in middle school because she'd gotten her period in the middle of class and was wearing yellow shorts.

"Hi, Cora." As usual, Sadie has possibly forgotten and most likely forgiven her.

"Congratulations. You, too, Jude. Don't let her get away."

I give Cora my best version of a smile when I really want to flip her off.

"I heard it was a beautiful ceremony," Cora says.

Is that some slight because she wasn't invited?

"It was. Thank you." Sadie's too gracious, if you ask me.

"I'm sure you were a gorgeous bride."

"Is," I correct.

"I'm sorry?" Cora says with a sweet voice that doesn't match her actual shit-talking gossipy mouth.

"She *is* a gorgeous bride," I clarify.

Sadie winds her arm through mine and tightens it as if telling me to stop talking.

"How long do you call her a bride for?" Cora looks at the other teller. She shrugs. "I guess she'll always be your bride."

Awkward silence fills the lobby. Actually, it's not awkward because I don't care, but Sadie's glaring arrows at me, so I guess she does.

"Is Mrs. Doyle available?" Sadie asks, apparently wanting to get out of this conversation.

"I'll get her," the other teller says.

"How's Bennett doing?" Cora asks.

Why the hell is she asking about my cousin—who is a lot younger than her?

"Fine," Sadie says, tilting her head, obviously wondering like me why she's asking.

"Wren is so cute. Our daughters are in the same class this year."

God help my cousin. I really hope the apple fell into the next farm over in that family.

"She's ready for you," the other teller says.

"Bye, guys. Good luck." Cora waves.

I catch the other teller going over to her as I wait for Sadie to enter Mrs. Doyle's office. Cora leans in but sees me looking and straightens her back. Yup. People don't change their spots.

"Sadie. Jude. I heard the news. Congratulations." Mrs. Doyle signals with her hand for us to sit in front of her.

"Thank you." Sadie sits in the farthest chair, and I sit beside her, reaching for her hand.

Mrs. Doyle clocks our hands and makes a small noise. "I'm assuming you're here to apply for the loan?"

"Yes. We brought our marriage license, and Jude has everything he needs."

Mrs. Doyle turns her attention to me. "Great. Glad this all worked out for you."

Her eyes shift to Sadie, and I'm not really thrilled by the

judgmental look on her face. But for now, I'll keep my mouth shut so I don't screw this up.

I lift my wrist. It's Monday, and although I'm technically off because of the wedding, I still don't want to be here all day.

"Let's get to the paperwork then." Mrs. Doyle turns to her computer.

Sadie glances at me, and I smile, squeezing her hand. She's got that look, as if questioning me if I really want to do this. That it's the last chance to say no. She's crazy if she thinks I wouldn't give her my last penny.

We go through the form, with me giving Mrs. Doyle most of the information—more than Sadie probably knows. My net worth is the biggest secret she probably had no idea about. She's unfazed when I tell Mrs. Doyle, so maybe she assumed. I don't know.

We both sign, and Mrs. Doyle says we should know in a few days.

"Bye, newlyweds!" Cora yells right before we walk out of the bank.

Sadie smiles and waves while I nod and open the doors for Sadie to go outside.

"Cora drives me fucking crazy," I say when we reach the sidewalk.

"She's not so bad."

"She's fake as shit. Bet she's talking shit about us to that other teller as we speak."

Sadie stops me at the front of my truck and fists my T-shirt. "Who cares what people think?"

She tugs me down, and I easily follow her direction, our lips meeting. Our kisses are becoming addictive, so I'm thankful she pulled me in instead of me always kissing her. We barely made it through breakfast without our lips attached to one another and our hands roaming. It's crazy to think how much the past twenty-four hours have changed my entire life.

"Let's go," I say, walking her to the passenger side of the truck.

Now we're off to her house to move her into mine. The sun gleams on my wedding band. I never thought I'd be a ring guy, but I kind of like looking at it and knowing Sadie gave it to me. Even if it was for a bullshit reason.

❧

WE DRIVE OVER TO SADIE'S COTTAGE, AND I PARK behind her cottage because it will be easier to move the stuff out the back door than the front.

"You know that day you were in a towel?" I ask, standing in the small hallway while she's in her bedroom, packing up the last of her clothes.

"Yeah?"

"Can we redo that day? You come out of the shower in a towel. I promise to make it worth your while." I lie on her bed, my hand running along her back as she sorts through her clothes.

"I don't know how much to bring."

"All of it." I scoot up and kiss her neck, trailing my way up to her earlobe.

"What are you doing?" she asks, continuing to fill her box.

"What do you think I'm doing?" I swing my leg on the other side of hers, straddling her from behind, and slide my hands up the hem of her shirt.

She leans back into me. "Distracting me. That's what you're doing."

But she doesn't fight me. She lets my hands glide up the sides of her stomach and wrap around her tits. I tug down the bra cups, rolling her nipples between my finger and thumb.

"Why don't you hike up that skirt?" I whisper before sucking on her earlobe.

She does as I ask, the free-flowing skirt making it easy for her to reveal herself to me. When I see her pink lace panties, my hand leaves her tit and drops to her thigh. Wanting her primed and ready, I tease her with barely a brush of my fingers on the outside of her underwear. She squirms in my arms, and I inch my hand up to the elastic waistband, then I slip my hand down the front. Her head falls to my shoulder on a sigh when I find her wet and ready for me.

"Jude." I love hearing her say my name when she's aroused. As if she's desperate for more of whatever I decide to give her.

"Do you want to come?" My finger dips between her folds.

"Yes."

I want that too because it's more beautiful than a sunset. I don't think I'll ever get enough of it now that I've had it—I'm a certified addict.

I inch a finger inside her, curling it upward as my thumb circles her clit, and she bucks against my hand. I plunge another finger inside her and kiss the shell of her ear, whispering about how wet she is and how badly I want her to fall apart on my fingers.

Her hips tilt up from the mattress, and I increase the pace. Her hand smashes down on my wrist as if she's afraid I'm going to stop. *Not on your life, babe.*

"Feel good?" I nibble on the shell of her ear.

She nods, turning her face toward mine. I capture her lips, my tongue plunging into her hot mouth. As our tongues tangle, neither of us is looking for dominance, just pleasure.

Seconds later, Sadie comes, and I swallow her cries as she stills with her hips in the air. I slow my pace, easing her down from the height of her orgasm. Her ass sinks back to the mattress, and I take my thumb off her clit, slowly withdrawing my fingers. Our kiss closes, and her head lolls to the side, a deep breath slipping from her lips.

"That was crazy," she says.

"I can't get enough of you." I kiss the nape of her neck before bringing my fingers up to my mouth and sucking her essence from them.

She watches me with heavy-lidded eyes. "My turn." Getting up, her skirt falls to just above her knees, and she kneels on the floor.

I place my hands on her shoulders. "At home."

God, that sounds good. Home. *Our* home.

"But—"

I shake my head. "Let's get your stuff."

I adjust myself—my poor dick is pressed against the zipper of my jeans. But I don't want her to think every time I give her an orgasm she's somehow required to reciprocate.

"I'm not going to forget. Tonight, it's your turn." She pokes my chest.

I grab her finger and tug her down on me. We kiss, and I roll us over so I'm on top, then I climb off her before we never leave this cottage.

She finishes packing while I cart her stuff to the truck.

"I'm going to go check on Mom," she says and heads past the cottage to her mom's back door.

After I shut the truck's tailgate, I go to follow her, but she opens the screen door and walks right back out. I stop where I am, a frown on my face. "What?"

"Um...we should go."

"Why?"

She grabs my hand and tugs me away from the stairs that lead into the house.

"Sadie!" her mom yells, coming to the screen door in a nightshirt. Her blonde hair is definitely messy as if she just woke up. "Get back here."

"Nope. That's okay."

"What am I missing?" I fight Sadie's tugging on my arm.

"Jude?" my dad's voice says. The back door opens, and my dad steps out without a shirt on.

"You have to be fucking kidding me," I say, my feet planted on the ground.

Chapter Twenty-Two

SADIE

"Will you two get in here?" Bruce walks right back through the screen door and into my parents' house.

Jude's eyebrows raise, and I walk past him.

"I don't want to know," Jude murmurs, but he follows me into the house.

My mom is at the stove, cutting up boiled eggs, a jar of mayonnaise next to her. Bruce is now at the table with a tall glass of iced tea in front of him. Still no shirt on, but at least he's wearing jeans.

"I don't want to open my eyes." Jude has his arm slung over his eyes. "Tell me you didn't?"

I assume that question is for Bruce.

"Stop being immature. You're thirty-four, for heaven's sake." Bruce isn't one to put up with antics, although Emmett gets away with a lot of crap.

I pull Jude's arm down from shielding his eyes, and he cracks one eye open to make sure it's safe.

"Can you please put on a shirt?" Jude says to his dad.

"Sorry, it was a rough morning. That's why I'm in my nightshirt. Last night drained all my energy," my mom says.

"We don't want details." I look between the two of them.

"Get your heads out of the gutter." Bruce gets up and disappears down the hall.

I turn to my mother. "Mom. Dad's only been gone for—"

"Sadie Ann. Don't you dare finish that sentence."

"But—"

"We did not sleep together." Bruce is putting on his plaid shirt as he walks back into the room.

"Go ahead and button that thing," Jude says.

"Then what's going on?" I ask, confused about this entire scene unfolding in front of me.

"Bruce is redoing the porch, putting in a ramp to make it easier for me to get in and out of the house. And I'm making him an egg salad sandwich for lunch." She lifts the bowl and shoots us a fake smile.

"Oh." My shoulders sag with guilt and maybe a little relief.

"I'm going to ignore the fact that you think I'd do that to your father." Mom spoons out a heap of mayo and drops it into the bowl.

"And one of my good friends," Bruce doubles down on making us feel guilty.

"Maybe if your Sunday Fundays weren't so blatant, Dad, we wouldn't be assuming." Jude crosses his arms.

"Why are you two here? You should be in bed," Mom says.

I glance at Jude with a mortified expression. Although, he did just give me an earth-shaking orgasm a half hour ago. "I'm packing."

"Oh good. I'll feed you guys some lunch. Sit."

"We weren't going to stay. I just wanted to check up on you." I remain standing because now that Jude and I have admitted our feelings, I really want to keep him to myself.

"Sit," Bruce says.

Jude groans, but we both know we're staying for lunch now. Jude walks around me and slides a chair out for me.

"We do have some news though," Bruce says as I sit down.

"What?" Jude acts like an annoyed teenager.

"Rhea is going to move in with me for a little while."

Jude sits in the chair next to me, and we share a look.

"Why?" I ask.

"I'm going to do some more intensive work on the house here. We're going to move her to the main floor, so she doesn't have to take the stairs, and I'm fixing the floor in here as well as on the porch. No point in her living downstairs if she falls through a loose board."

"Oh."

"I told Bruce I was fine, but now with you moving in with Jude..."

I don't love my mom being on the ranch all by herself with no one else around. I'm close enough I suppose, but I still don't love the idea.

"Are you sure, Mom?" I ask.

"Bruce offered me a permanent spot on the land now that you're married. There's a parcel of land we could build a house on, but I want to stay on the farm." She puts a few slices of bread in the toaster. "I don't want to leave."

"But maybe you should." I give her a look I hope reads as "at least consider it."

"You're welcome to move in with us," Jude says.

I don't do a good job of hiding my shocked expression.

My mom laughs. "I would never intrude, but thank you for the offer. I've been feeling really good lately. Maybe the stress of the farm finances being lifted is helping me. How is the chicken farm idea going anyway?" She hands Bruce his sandwich and pops another two slices of bread into the toaster.

"We went to the bank today." Jude eyes his dad, and Bruce

nods. "Once we get the money and pay off the back mortgage, it's really just making the chicken coops and finding the chicks to start the first batch in late February or March. It might take a little while, but Sadie's done her legwork on what we need to do."

I reach over and Jude meets me halfway, holding my hand on the table.

Bruce's eyes land on our hands, and he smirks. "That's good to hear. We'll harvest the soybeans next week, I think." His eyes focus on Jude since Jude's probably going to be the one managing it.

"That will help with start-up costs," I say. "Thank you."

There's a beat of silence, then Bruce says, "I'm going to have Emmett do the corn maze this year."

Jude's hand goes limp over mine. "What? Why?"

"You're a newlywed, and you have a lot on your plate."

My mom brings another sandwich over, putting it in front of Jude, who keeps his eyes on his dad as he slides the plate over to me without even looking in my direction.

"I do the maze every year. Emmett's going to do a penis or something."

"Give me some credit. I'd do a vulva." Emmett shows up through the doorway from the family room.

I startle, but I'm the only one.

"What the hell are you doing here?" Jude asks.

"Dad needed more wood. I make deliveries now." Emmett squeezes Jude's shoulders before Jude slides out of his grip. "Looking good, Mrs. Wilkins." He kisses my mom on the cheek.

"Sit down, Emmett. I'll make you a sandwich," Mom says. She's always had a soft spot for Emmett. Probably because he was a baby when their mom died, and Mom always gave him extra hugs and kisses since she knew he'd never remember Mrs. Noughton.

"I'm doing the maze," Jude says with a tone that brokers no argument.

"Come on, bossman, time to hand over the reins." Emmett leans back on his chair, teetering on the two back legs.

"I've already sketched it out."

Bruce and Emmett raise their eyebrows at each other, though I don't know why. Jude is the hardest working guy I know.

"Fine. You can do the maze, you baby," Emmett says with an eye roll.

"If you run yourself too thin—" I start.

"I won't," Jude says, looking at me. "You could ride with me and keep me company."

As if I'd ever say no to spending a day with Jude.

"No, no, no. No one wants to see your naked asses in the tractor." Emmett waves his hands. "Who will disinfect it when you're done?"

"That job goes to the low man on the ladder—you." Jude laughs.

Even Bruce stares at Jude as if he doesn't recognize him. Usually, Jude would just tell Emmett to fuck off.

My mom brings my sandwich but sees I already have one since Jude gave me his. She bends and kisses his cheek, putting the sandwich in front of him.

"Where's my lovin'?" Emmett asks.

My mom shoos him with her hand. "You're not why my daughter looks like she's flying high on helium." She runs her hand down my hair before going back to prepare more sandwiches, because we both know one isn't enough for these boys.

I stand, grab some more eggs, and take them over for my mom. "You sit, I'll finish."

She pats my hand. "Thank you."

"Don't forget we've got softball on Thursday," Emmett

says. "Rumor has it Walker is going to scout the team we're playing. They're new this year. Horse Haven. They take in old racehorses. Non-profit."

It always amazes me how much Emmett can seem like a goof, but the research he does on the rival ranches' softball teams is always impressive. Especially when you consider that if you win the season, all you get is a trophy.

Jude stands and meets me at the counter. "You go eat." His hand wraps around my waist, his mouth so close to my ear that I wish we were alone again.

"It will go faster together." I smile at him, but my gaze snags on the table.

Three sets of eyes are all concentrated on us.

Mom's got a goofy smile.

Bruce has a satisfied grin.

And Emmett's eyebrows are furrowed.

I'm sure they don't all believe that our marriage was for love. Jude has never acted like this with me before. This means we were probably doing a poor job of convincing people. Now things are different, but at some point, do people need to know that we got into this marriage to secure a loan?

Have we confused things with the newfound relationship we slipped into last night? Do I even care? We're married but haven't even had a real date. Just when I get what I want, I get it with complications I'm not sure how to unknot.

Chapter Twenty-Three

I shower, dry myself, and wrap the towel around my waist before walking into my bedroom...er, our bedroom. Sadie isn't here. She told me she was going to lie down, so I expected she'd be in our bed.

Leaving my room, I go in search of her. She's asleep in the guest bedroom. I stand in the doorway, admiring the way her hands are tucked under her cheek and how peaceful she looks. Her long blonde hair is strewn across the pillow. I can't believe she's here. With me. But what is she doing in the guest room?

I walk in and slide my hands under her neck and legs, picking her up.

Her eyes slowly open. "What are you doing?"

"Taking you to my bed." I carry her bride-style, side-stepping through the doorway, and lay her on the bed. "*This* is your bed."

She smiles and sits up, her eyes tracing over my body. Her finger slips below the towel at my waist. "Did I offend you?"

"No." My stomach sucks in, and my breath hitches, having her fingers running the length of my waist. My dick twitches and tents the towel.

"Okay, good." She grabs the end of the towel tucked inside and pulls it free. The towel falls to the floor, and I stand there naked with my dick pointing north. "I think someone wants to play."

"He's had a lot of time at the playground the last few days."

"There's a new ride." She scoots to the end of the bed, her feet falling to the floor.

"What's it called?"

"We haven't named it yet." She pretends to think, her mouth twisting. "But I think he's going to love it." Her fingers rake down my chest, and she lightly pushes me.

I stumble, my back hitting the wall behind me.

"I think he is too." My voice is raspy.

She kisses my shoulder before she trails her lips down my abdomen. Her eyes are on mine, and a devilish smile is plastered on her pouty pink lips. Her fingernails run down my thighs, wrapping around to my ass as she falls to her knees, coming face to face with my dick.

"Well, hello there." Her tongue licks my tip.

I pile her blonde hair in my hand, twisting it around my fist so I can watch.

She flattens her tongue and runs it up my length and back down. "You're so eager today."

Licking me again while pumping her fist at my base, she circles her tongue as though she's lapping up ice cream from a cone, then she swallows down the tip of my cock. Fuck. My dick hits the back of her throat, and she pops it back out.

Looking up at me again, she says, "Enjoy the ride."

She grips my base hard, and my dick twitches in her palm. She takes me into her mouth again, her tongue swirling, her fist pumping. A beautiful flush covers her body, and I can't stop watching her, my dick growing harder with every tug.

Her hand remains on my base, holding me steady as she

sucks me down her throat. My head falls back to the wall, and my hand tightens her strands. I want to touch her, feast on her, fuck her, but she's hell-bent on making me come with her mouth. I don't blame her. I fucking love it when I make her come. It's my new addiction.

When I'm already practically there, trying my hardest to push my orgasm away, her other hand comes into play as though she knows where I'm at. Cupping my balls, massaging them, she sucks me so good I can barely keep my eyes open to watch her.

"Fuck," I rasp. "I love this ride."

Her eyes are wide, looking up at me, and witnessing my cock down her throat finishes me off.

"I'm gonna come," I groan.

She nods slightly, mumbling something I can't understand. Her hands wind around and grab my ass, pulling me further into her mouth, my dick breaching the back of her throat. My hands release her hair and move to the sides of her face, and I fuck her mouth twice before I can't hold back, still inside her warm wet heat, and come in her mouth.

She slowly releases my dick, lapping up the mess before falling back onto her ankles. "I do hope you enjoyed the ride and will come back and see us again soon."

She kisses the tip, but I'm still in a daze, trying to recover from the best blow job I've ever gotten. "Hell, I'm gonna buy him a season's pass."

She chuckles, and I reach for her. She rises to her feet and comes toward me. I grip the back of her head and kiss her thoroughly, tasting myself on her tongue.

"I guess you have to take another shower," she says when we pull apart.

I pick her up and carry her into my bathroom. "It's time for your ride."

After turning on the water, I drop her to her feet, strip her down, and carry her into the shower, where I press her to the wall, throw one of her legs over my shoulders, and feast on her.

I'm in deep, and I don't even give a shit because after all these years, it's like having the entire playground to myself to explore over and over again.

👛

WE ARRIVE AT THE FIELD EARLY SO I CAN GET IT ready since we're the home team. I told my dipshit brothers to meet me here, but neither are around.

"I got you something," I say, walking over to the baseball field.

"A present?" Sadie turns to me, all giddy and excited.

"Nothing big. Just so everyone knows who you're here to cheer for."

She shakes her head with a smile as we enter the dugout. "I'm pretty sure everyone knows."

I guide her over to the bench and pull the T-shirt out of my bag. I would've given it to her at home, but I had to pick her up from her cottage because she was working on the branding for her new chicken farm. I told her she can work from the house, but she insists she's more focused there, and it'll let her keep an eye on her mom once the renovations on the main house are done.

She lifts the Plain Daisy Ranch softball shirt we all wear. On the back it says Jude's Girl with the number one under it. "Aw...I love it."

She wraps her arms around me, and I swing my arm around her waist, pulling her tight against me.

"Good. Now, let's get it on before anyone else arrives." I snag the hem of her T-shirt, dragging it up her torso.

She gasps. "Not here. What if someone comes?"

"They're always late, and it'll take two seconds."

She steps back and allows me to remove her T-shirt. Her bra is sheer blue, and I can see her nipples. I bend down and suck one into my mouth.

She hits my back. "Jude!"

"No fear, Sadie, Emmett's here." He jumps out from behind the corner, and Sadie yelps, pushing me back and covering herself. "Oh, shit!" Emmett cracks up, bending over at the waist, but he doesn't leave.

"Get the fuck outta here," I shout.

"Honestly, it's like envisioning Dad fucking. I just can't." He covers his eyes and walks away. I'm not sure who else has arrived, but I hear him say, "Don't go over there. Sadie and Jude are getting it on."

Sadie rips the shirt from my hold and throws it over her head. "I told you."

I grab her arm, tugging her back to me. "Sorry, that bra is just so fucking sexy."

She easily forgives me, allowing me to give her a kiss that lasts a little too long.

"We're going to revisit this later," I say to her back as she walks out of the dugout.

"Depends how you play." She gives me a cheeky smile before disappearing around the corner.

Emmett returns a minute later. "I think there needs to be a rule about no fraternizing in the dugouts. This is a common area, and my mental game is now ruined because I have to envision you sucking on Sadie's nipple." Emmett drops his bag and sits down to pout in the corner.

"Grow up." Ben kicks Emmett's feet, and Emmett slides them back to let Ben through. "Things are good with the married couple then?"

"Perfect."

"I figured, since everyone says you're never around after hours now, and your lunches are hours long."

I fight my smirk because I've never enjoyed lunch more than this week. "Stay out of my business."

I grab my clipboard to write down the lineup for today. Usually, it'd already be done, but I've been in Sadieville lately.

"I saw the T-shirt." Ben crosses his arms. "I want one for Gillian."

I shrug. "Sorry, last one they had." I concentrate on the lineup.

"Bullshit. If you don't get me one of those with Ben's Girl on the back, I'm going to strike out at every bat."

He's such an asshole, using his athletic ability as leverage. He pretty much hits a home run at every fucking game.

"I'll see what I can do." I turn away.

One by one, my cousins arrive, each one dressed in shorts and a T-shirt. The other team arrives and warms up in the field area. They're new to our softball league, but I know some of them. They're good people, taking in racehorses after they've retired. Finding them non-racing families to take care of them. But if we're going to beat our nemesis, Wild Bull Ranch, and shove it up Walker Matthews's ass, we have to beat Horses Haven.

"I'm not sure any of them can catch." Ben watches them with me, and he's right. Their throws aren't great, and their catches are worse.

"Should be a piece of cake," Emmett says, tossing a ball in the air and catching it. Sometimes I wonder when he'll grow up. He throws it up for the tenth time.

Female laughter rings out from the stands, and Emmett looks over. The ball hits him in the forehead.

"I might not need you today, but I'm gonna need you to beat Wild Bull," I say.

Emmett looks at the bleachers again and bends over to pick up the ball before rushing over to us. "Who's that blonde?"

"My wife," I say. "She's hot, right? Comes to all the games, so keep your fucking hands to yourself."

He rolls his eyes. "If I wanted Sadie, I would've stolen her right from under your nose. You know, when you were in the dark about your feelings for her?"

I push him with my hand.

"It's Briar," Ben says.

"Briar who?" Emmett asks, forehead wrinkled. Ben pushes Emmett's chest, and Emmett exaggerates his reaction, stumbling back. "You're always picking on me."

"Gillian's half sister. How many Briars do you know?" I ask.

He shakes his head. "That's not her."

I step out and wave to Sadie as though I'm checking in. Sure enough, Briar, Gillian's younger half sister, is sitting in the stands with all the women. "That's her."

"I drove her here, so I'm pretty sure it's her." Ben shakes his head, grabbing his bat.

Ben steps out, winks at Gillian, and takes practice swings. The man is so competitive. I guess we all are, but he takes it to the next level. Maybe it's the professional sports thing.

"What's up, boys?" Our friend Brooks walks up sporting a blinding pair of short white pants with socks and a belt that matches our shirt.

"FYI, the MLB didn't call," Lottie sneers at him.

"Are you trying to be recruited by the Wild Bull Ranch?" Romy asks, looking him over.

"You have to look the part." Brooks puffs out his chest.

"Okay, then." I shake my head at him.

"It's a good thing Lottie's wearing sweats tonight, so you won't ruin your brand-new pants." Ben stops swinging and pats Brooks on the shoulder.

"Coaches!" the ump calls.

I step out of the dugout and stop for a second. Walker

Matthews is sitting right next to Sadie, chatting her up. What the fuck is with that?

I walk over to the ump and the other coach, trying to pay attention, but when Sadie laughs, my fists clench in my pockets.

"We're away," I say to the ump.

"Home coach," the umpire corrects me.

"Home, I mean." I shake my head, trying to act unfazed.

I don't want to seem jealous. And truth is, Sadie isn't going to go for a class-A asshole like Walker Matthews. Then again, she is in love with me. So what does that say?

Chapter Twenty-Four

SADIE

I've sat on these bleachers many times. I've admired Jude playing softball and being the leader of his team. But it's different this time. I'm here as Jude's wife. Although I wear a ring on my left hand and on paper we're married, it's really just a beginning for us.

"So, Briar, why are you back in town?" Walker asks Gillian's sister.

He's so close I can smell his peppermint breath from the amount of gum he chews. Why is he sitting next to me? Walker's family owns Wild Bull Ranch, the second biggest ranch in Nebraska next to Plain Daisy Ranch, but since he took it over, he's been trying to make it bigger and better.

"I'm just visiting." She smiles sweetly at him.

Briar is eight years younger than Gillian, which seemed like a much bigger difference when Gillian used to watch her in high school, but now Briar's all grown up.

"That's cool. How long are you staying?" Walker asks.

Briar glances at Gillian, and Gillian puts her hand on her sister's knee and says, "As long as she wants."

They share a look as if there's more than they're willing to say in front of everyone.

"I don't want to intrude too long," Briar says.

"You can intrude at my place," Walker says with a smile.

Gillian shoots him a look over her shoulder.

None of us are big fans of Walker. He's not just cocky, he's arrogant and can't keep his mouth shut.

"She'll come to my place if that's the case." Laurel puts her arm around Briar, and Briar leans her head on her shoulder.

My phone pings, and I grab it out of my purse, silencing it before checking to see who sent me a message. It's from Melody, my good friend from high school.

> I'm coming into town two days early. Want to meet up for dinner?

I talk to Melody a few times a year, and we keep up on each other's lives. We were pretty competitive in high school with our grades, and we shared a passion for getting out of this town for bigger and better things. But senior year, my mom fell ill, and they couldn't diagnose her with anything definitive, so I stayed back while Melody went to a big school in California. Now she's a defense attorney and has even been on the news a few times.

I hammer back a text.

> I'd love to catch up!

The three dots appear immediately. With all the chaos of the wedding, I forgot about our fifteen-year class reunion in a few weeks. I didn't want to go when I got the invitation in the mail, but now it doesn't sound so bad. I had a lot of fun with Melody.

Great. I'll message you next week. I can't
wait to see you!

I text back that I'm excited too, and we'll talk soon.

Jude steps up to bat, and I shove the phone back into my purse.

"Go Jude!" I clap, and he turns to me, winking.

"You guys are the real thing, huh?" Walker asks me.

"Yes," I answer without taking my eyes off Jude.

He slides the bat along the home plate and gets in his stance, his ass out and strong arms up, holding the bat. A pitch comes in and is way right. Not even close to being over the plate.

Walker makes a noise as if it's breezing by.

The next pitch comes in, and it almost hits Jude.

Walker groans. "Not sure they should be in our league."

"It's not the majors," Laurel says. "It's recreational softball."

"All sports are competitive. That's the whole point."

"Apparently because you have nothing better to do than scout a team you're playing next week." Gillian lobs the insult over her shoulder.

"Exactly." He smacks his gum.

I miss the pitch but hear the bat connect to a ball. I look up as the ball drops between center and left field. Jude gets on base with a double.

I'm on my feet in an instant. "Woohoo! Go, Jude!"

Emmett steps out of the dugout. "Calm down there, Sadie. The real Noughton is up to bat now." He scans the bleachers and stops on Briar for a beat longer than everyone else.

"I hate cocky guys," Briar says, leaning back to rest her arms on the bleacher behind her.

The first pitch comes across the plate. Emmett swings and misses.

"Thanks for the breeze, Noughton," Walker shouts.

Emmett doesn't look up, shaking his head. The dugout cheers him on, Lottie's voice the loudest. The second pitch comes in, and he swings and misses again.

"That felt good," Walker continues to razz him, and all of us give Walker a dirty look.

Emmett gets ready again, swings, and misses on the third pitch, striking out. He hammers the bat on the ground and heads back into the dugout. Brooks pats him on the shoulder, standing in the warm-up box while Ben steps up to the plate.

Ben looks at Gillian. "Home run?"

"Or nothing," she says.

They both laugh.

"Ew, was that some kind of sexual reference?" Briar asks, her nose scrunching.

Laurel and I laugh.

"One day you'll get it." Gillian pats her knee and swings her arm around her, pulling her in.

The game continues, and by the fourth inning, Plain Daisy is slaughtering Horses Haven. We're all bored, even the players.

"I've got nothing to be worried about." Walker stands and steps down the bleachers. "See you guys later."

We all share a look, happy he's leaving. Then Scarlett comes up to bat. The poor girl doesn't get a lot of hits, but she might be the most competitive player.

"Actually." Walker sits down on the bottom bleacher. "Eye on the ball, Scar."

She turns around and narrows her eyes. Wiggling her ass, she gets ready in the batter's box. The first pitch comes in, and she hits a ground ball that moves Bennett to third, where he slides. The ball gets thrown to first base before Scarlett makes it there.

"You don't have to slide every time!" Jude yells at his cousin.

"They almost got me," he shouts back, and we all laugh.

Scarlett walks back toward the dugout, and Walker steps up to the fence, linking his fingers through the openings. "I'm available for private lessons."

"Go to hell," she says and disappears into the dugout.

He finally leaves.

Plain Daisy Ranch ends up beating Horses Haven twenty-four to nothing. After the game, the Noughton family and Brooks collect all their things while we sit in the bleachers and gossip.

"I've heard so many people are coming back for the reunion," Laurel says. "Are you excited?"

Let's be honest, most people we graduated with still live in Willowbrook or a nearby town, but a few live outside Nebraska.

"Funny you say that. Melody just messaged me during the game to get together while she's here," I say.

"Oh really? I figured she'd never come back. I saw that documentary the other day where she was the lawyer. Seems she's doing really well for herself," Gillian says.

Melody really did make it big.

The boys all come join us, Jude walking right over to me and Ben going to Gillian. Emmett hovers, his gaze bouncing to Briar every few seconds. I've never seen him this quiet.

"What about you, Jude?" Laurel asks. "Excited for the reunion?"

He grunts and puts his arm around me. "I wasn't planning on going."

I place my hand on his stomach and look up at him. "You weren't?"

"I think you're going now." Ben laughs.

Jude frowns. "You really want to go? We already see everyone."

"Not everyone, and Melody is coming back."

A look crosses his face that I can't figure out the meaning of.

"I hate her. Remember when she was the hall monitor or whatever? Now she defends criminals. How does that make sense?" Emmett finally says something, but he's still more subdued than normal.

"Everyone is innocent until proven guilty." Briar crosses her arms and juts out her hip.

"What's up, Briar?" Emmett nods, his cockiness slowly returning.

"Not much, little Noughton."

We all share a look, wondering if we're missing something.

"Let's go home." Jude ushers me toward his truck.

"No drinks at The Hidden Cave?" Ben shouts.

"I think he's got his own entertainment now," Emmett says.

We ignore them and walk to Jude's truck. I'll never get used to that word when it comes to Jude and me. Home. Maybe dreams do come true.

Chapter Twenty-Five

JUDE

It's been a few weeks since the wedding, and we got the loan, so we've been concentrating on getting the land ready before winter comes in full force. My dad and some of our employees harvested the soybeans since I have to do the corn maze and some other things around the ranch. Emmett was supposed to be in charge of harvesting, and from what some of the employees said, he did a good job. Hopefully, he'll take a little of the load off me.

I'm dreading tonight, though. Melody Klein from high school is coming to my house—not only for dinner, but Sadie invited her to stay here. She's cleaned our house from top to bottom, scrubbing floors and sweeping off the porch. Melody's parents moved to Los Angeles once she became a big deal and had kids so they could be closer to her, which means Melody doesn't really know anyone in town anymore.

"I'm running out of time to get this meal cooked." Sadie cuts up the chicken to bread it and fry. "Can you sit down and check the graphics I did?" She points toward her computer and the few marketing sheets next to where she was working today.

I wrap my arms around her stomach, sliding her hair over and kissing her neck. "Calm down. It's going to be great."

"I'm nervous now that she's going to be staying here. I feel like I don't really know her anymore, you know? It's been years since I've seen her. I was different then."

I continue to trail kisses up her shoulder and neck, my hands weaving under her apron, unbuttoning her blouse.

"Jude," she says, but doesn't stop me.

"Let me relax you," I whisper, sliding my hand through an opening and cupping her tit. I love how responsive she is when I touch her.

"I'm not sure when she's coming, and I have chicken hands." She raises her gloved hands.

"Then allow me." My hands go down to her pants, and I unbutton them, pulling the zipper down. Snaking my hand under the waistband of her underwear, I find her wet and ready. "Someone's primed."

Her head falls to my shoulder, and I nip at her neck. She says my name, and my dick grows in my jeans. I love when she says my name like that. When I slide my finger over her clit, she moans, her mouth casting kisses to my jaw. I capture her lips in a searing kiss that only spurs the want inside me.

"Sadie?" A knock sounds on the screen door.

She whips her head around so fast, pulling her lips off mine, that her head hits me in the jaw.

"Fuck." My hand slides out from her pants, and I cup my jaw, opening and moving it around.

"I'm sorry," she says, going to touch me, but I hold her wrists before she touches me with chicken hands. Her cheeks are pink. I love that look on her.

"It's fine. I'll let her in." I kiss Sadie's forehead and walk around the island.

Melody stands outside the screen door in what I'm pretty sure is an expensive pantsuit. Her dark hair is styled as though she had it professionally done, and it's clear she doesn't fit in in Willowbrook anymore.

"Jude Noughton." She giggles, though I'm not sure what's so funny.

I open the door. "Hi, Melody."

"Hi, Melody." She imitates me in a voice that doesn't sound anything like me.

I'm already irritated.

She walks into my house, wheeling her suitcase behind her and placing it by the front door. It's a reminder that she'll be here when I wake up. The only saving grace is that she was supposed to stay for longer, but some big case took longer than she expected or some shit. She's here for two nights. Tonight and tomorrow, the night of the reunion.

"This place is so cute. Farmhouse modern is what they call it, I think."

I inwardly groan and turn on a fake smile because her impression of me means something to Sadie.

"Jude built it himself." Sadie comes from behind me and joins us. She's all put back together. Her blouse is buttoned up, her pants secure, and I stuff my hands into my pockets.

"Oh, you always were so handy." Melody laughs, but it doesn't come near to reaching her eyes. "Sadie, you look fabulous. Small town life looks good on you."

She opens her arms and swarms Sadie in a hug while the words *small town life looks good on you* raise my blood pressure.

"You look like you stepped out of a magazine." Sadie steps back and holds Melody's hands out to look at her. "You're a mother of three? I'd never guess."

Melody waves. "Well, Dave gifted me a tummy tuck after the third. It was my push gift."

"Push gift?" I ask, cursing myself in my head for even asking. I plan on eating dinner with them, then going upstairs for the night, letting them catch up. I've never cared for Melody.

"Do you guys have those here? The husband gets the wife a gift for having the baby."

"Isn't the baby the gift?"

Sadie shoots me a look to be quiet and not judge.

"Well, you look great. Come on in. Do you want some wine?" Sadie waves her into the kitchen.

"Do you mind if I change? I had to go to the airport right from the courthouse, and I feel disgusting. Jude, do you mind taking my suitcase to my room?"

Sadie shoots me another "be nice" look.

"Sure." I pick it up and walk up the stairs, then put it in the spare room. I turn around to leave, but she's there, peeking into the room.

"Oh great, is there a shower in here too?" she asks.

"Down the hall," I say, pointing toward the bathroom the other three bedrooms share.

She giggles again. "I forgot how traditional all the houses are around here. Dave and I put bathrooms in each of our kids' bedrooms. Makes it easier."

I don't give a shit.

"Awesome. Towels are under the sink." I step out of the room while she comes in, and we end up sliding against one another.

"You must be happy, huh?"

I turn back toward her from the top of the stairs. "What do you mean?"

"It all worked out for you."

I turn to face her directly. "What did?"

"That Sadie couldn't go away. I mean, she should be with me in Los Angeles or in New York or some other big city. For you, it's probably good that she had to stay back here to care for her mom."

My jaw sets. "What are you implying?"

She giggles for I swear the hundredth time since she walked into my house. "Always so serious. I didn't mean anything by it. I just meant it all worked out. You two are married."

My thumb runs over my ring—as it often does when I wonder how it has all worked out. That Sadie is my wife. A dream I never thought would happen. But we've been happy since the wedding, and I only fall more in love with her every day.

"If you need anything, let us know." I climb down the stairs and go to the kitchen.

Surely I can keep it together for forty-eight hours.

SADIE MAKES AN AMAZING GARLIC BUTTER CHICKEN with spinach and bacon in a cast iron pan, serving it over pasta. I'm on my second plate when Melody asks about the farm. Or, as she puts it, "farm life."

"I'm turning my family farm into a free-range chicken farm." Sadie sounds so proud. "Jude's already built one of the coops, and this winter, we're going to get everything else ready."

Melody sips her wine, only eating a quarter of her plate. "That's so cute. I can see you out there, sprinkling food out of your apron with all the chickens around your ankles."

Sadie laughs. "Well, it won't be that small of an operation."

"But starting out, it will be, no?" Melody asks. She always has a smile to mask her insults.

"Depends on how many chicks we get. Jude and I still have to work out some of the logistics." Sadie refills their glasses. "Do you need another beer, Jude?"

"I'm good, thanks."

"You're such a good little wife. I sit on the couch and have Dave get my drinks." Melody laughs.

Sadie doesn't say anything to that, and I'm growing more annoyed by the second. I pile another forkful of food in my mouth to make sure I don't say something to embarrass Sadie.

Melody looks at the edge of the table and picks up a piece of paper, which she has no business doing, but I have a feeling she doesn't really respect boundaries. "These are adorable. Did you do this?" She holds up the branding sheet Sadie wanted me to look at earlier but got distracted by, well, her. "I'd buy your eggs or chicken with this logo and branding."

Sadie tries to tame her smile by biting her lip, but I can tell it means a lot to her that Melody likes her concept. "Thanks. I've been tweaking it for weeks."

"I stopped at The Harvest Depot on my way in to say hello to Lottie, and she said you did most of the logos for the products they sell. You're actually really talented."

Of course she is. How can someone say something nice, but still make it sound underhanded?

"Packaging sells," Sadie says with a smile.

"That's the truth. I've been fooled a lot of times by talented people like you." She laughs and tips back her wine.

We finish dinner, and I tell Sadie I'll clean up while they go out on the porch to catch up.

"Thanks." She kisses my cheek, grabbing a bottle of wine, and heads outside.

"I can't get over how cute this all is. You live such a low-key life. I'm jealous," Melody says, and I grunt, taking my aggression out on the dishes. "Everything is go, go, go in Los Angeles. Dave and I have to schedule date nights three times a week. Thank god for the nanny."

After I clean up the kitchen, I wipe down the table and counters. With the windows open, I can hear them talking.

Sadie tells Melody about her dad dying, her mom's health, and almost losing the farm. She's honest and raw, not hiding her emotions. It's so admirable that I want to go out there and hug her for being such an amazing person.

Melody carries on about Dave and how much they both work. She talks about being thankful she's done having kids so young, and although it was hard to have them back-to-back-to-back, she's glad she won't be an old mom.

Everyone who knows Sadie knows she wants a family, so I don't know why Melody's going on like that in front of her.

"What about you and Jude? Kids?" Melody asks.

I eavesdrop because we haven't had that type of discussion about our future. We're technically married, but that arrangement was made before we were an actual couple. We're in this weird limbo state, and we've been so distracted by each other that we haven't decided what to do moving forward.

"Oh, I don't know. We just got married." It's the first time tonight that Sadie's stalled as if she's unsure how to answer.

"Would Jude ever leave Willowbrook?"

"I don't think so. He runs Plain Daisy's cattle ranch. His life is definitely here."

"Too bad because I have a friend I know would love your artistic skills. You have a real eye, Sadie. You know that, right? I can't help but feel like you're wasting it here."

There's a pause before Sadie answers. "I'm not wasting it. I'm creating my own company."

"Remember all the dreams you had? All the times we talked about living in an apartment in a big city? We'd be rich and powerful women breaking those glass ceilings. I just—"

"I'm happy," Sadie says, but her tone isn't as convincing as I wish it was.

"I get that you scored Jude after all these years and that makes you happy, but are you sure you're not going to wake up in ten years regretting that you never got out of this town?"

I lean back against the wall, waiting for her to answer. My gut twists because as much as I don't like Melody, she has a point. At some stage in Sadie's life, she's going to mourn that she never accomplished all she was meant to in this life. I don't like the idea of her sacrificing her happiness, then resenting me for it.

"I told you. I'm happy," Sadie repeats. I worry she's trying to convince herself as much as she's trying to convince Melody.

Chapter Twenty-Six

SADIE

The reunion was fun, but Melody has been driving me a little crazy since she got here, and Jude has spoken to me many times about his dislike of her. He's being a good husband, keeping his mouth shut, but it's about time I set it straight with Melody, even if she's not going to be a part of our daily lives.

She comes down the stairs, dressed in a leisure-type purple pantsuit. Jude already brought her suitcase down this morning before he headed out.

"It's been so much fun catching up. Thanks for letting me stay. It's not like Willowbrook has any four-star hotels," Melody laughs, slamming the town that raised her again. One for the road, I guess.

"You know, Melody, I really am happy here."

She runs her hand down my upper arm. "I know you are. But you must—"

"No." I shake my head. "I'm *really* happy here. I've found myself, and sure, what I wanted in high school seemed so big and amazing, but I'm not sure it was ever for me. I know my life seems small to you, but it's not. I have Jude, who adores me. I'm close to my mom. I have friends who are always there for me. And I'm going to have a great chicken farm."

"I never meant to—"

"I'm sure you didn't. But the little digs that somehow my life isn't what I want is hurtful. To not only me, but Jude. I made my choice a long time ago. I'm not that eighteen-year-old anymore. It's great that you're happy in Los Angeles, and you're living the life that we dreamed of, but my dreams changed. And that's okay."

Melody nods, frowning. "I just remember us saying how we were gonna have it all. A career and a family and money, and we'd go out for drinks and fancy dinners."

She literally lives the life we said we wanted, but hearing her talk about her life is exhausting. It sounds kind of empty. I like sitting on the porch and watching the ducks with Jude, talking about nothing and everything. I like Friday night football games in the fall where I know everyone and the corn maze every Halloween, pig roasts on the Fourth of July here on the ranch. The endless parades. I even enjoy walking down the sidewalk downtown and running into people I've known my entire life, even if I resent their interest in my personal affairs sometimes.

"And I'm happy you got it. But it's not for me."

She's quiet for a moment. "I'm sorry. I really didn't mean any harm. I just...this small town living isn't my thing."

I smile. "I know, and that's okay."

She opens her arms. "Hug it out?"

"Of course."

We wrap our arms around each other, and I squeeze her tightly because I have a feeling this could be the last time I see her. This short visit confirmed that we're different people now.

"Maybe when you have that chicken farm going, I'll bring the kids for a visit."

She won't.

"You're always welcome."

Just don't ask Jude.

We step away from one another and share a smile.

"Have a safe trip home," I say.

"Thank Jude for me?"

"I will."

I open the screen door, and she walks out and down the stairs to her Uber ride. I watch her leave. She doesn't give me one last wave through the back window, and that's okay. She was okay leaving Willowbrook in her rearview mirror, but it's her loss.

I want to have a little alone time with Jude after our visitor, so I go inside, put together a lunch, and hop in the UTV, driving out to the corn field.

He's beside the tractor, looking at his papers, when he hears me. The smile that splits his lips is the exact reason I came out here.

"What are you doing here?" he asks, deserting his papers and hugging me, kissing my temple.

"I wanted to see you." I lift the cooler I packed. "And I brought you lunch."

"You could be my lunch." He backs me up against the tractor, caging me in.

"That sounds good too. Should we go home?"

"I've got a better plan." He grabs the papers and climbs up on the tractor. His GPS screen hangs from the front. "Ride with me."

I grab the lunch cooler and accept his offered hand. I sit on his lap, and he starts the tractor, driving it through the corn maze until we're driving through eight-foot corn stalks.

"It's kind of creepy in here," I say.

"I'll keep you safe."

He stops us a good way in where he still has to plow, so

that we're surrounded by vegetation. "We're gonna have to be resourceful here." He kisses my neck. "Straddle me. And lift that dress."

I'm wearing more dresses now because Jude loves them, and it makes it so easy to fool around since we can't seem to keep our hands off one another. We're certainly making up for lost time.

I swing my leg over his lap, but he holds me steady on my hips. "Get me out."

I smile at his order, and my hands go to his belt buckle. I've mastered undoing his belt and pants since our wedding. I slide down his pants and pull his dick out of his boxer briefs. The sight of it standing thick, tall, and proud makes me wet. We haven't had sex in two days since Melody was here. I stayed up late with her both nights, and Jude went to bed since he gets up so early.

He runs his finger between my legs. "How are you already wet?"

"I feel like I'm always wet around you."

"Such a great problem to have." He smirks and eases me down on him.

I sink down, and he fills me inch by inch until he's fully seated inside me. God, I missed this so much. I place my hands on his shoulders and grind my hips forward and back.

"Shit, you feel amazing, Sadie."

"So do you." I inch forward, pressing my lips to his.

We spend the next fifteen minutes having fun in the tractor in the middle of the corn maze field. I'll never look at it the same again. Then afterward, I feed him lunch and spend my afternoon plowing the corn maze with him.

Melody has no idea what she's missing. Farm life is incredible.

❧

JUDE LEAVES BEFORE THE SUN IS FULLY UP. I HATE waking up without him, but that's the life of a farmer's wife. I run my hand over Jude's pillow and find a bouquet of wild-flowers and a note.

I sit up and open the envelope. His scribbled handwriting warms my chest.

> Sadie,
> Date night. Be ready at six.
>
> Yours,
> Jude

We're finally going on a real date. Not just pizza or ice cream or one of us making dinner. We've been so busy with everything that we haven't gone on an actual date, and I'm so excited. I pick up the bouquet of flowers and hold them to my chest. Could life be any better? I don't think so.

When the scent of the flowers hits my nostrils, nausea gurgles in my stomach. I gag on vomit rising up my throat.

Tossing the flowers aside, I run to the bathroom, falling to my knees and wrapping my arms around the porcelain toilet. For a moment, the nausea settles, but a second later, it rushes back, and I throw up in the toilet. By the time I'm done, my throat burns, and I sit back on my heels. My stomach feels a little better now. I touch my forehead, wondering if I'm coming down with something, but I'm not clammy or hot.

"What the hell?" I say, flushing the toilet and standing.

I turn on the shower, rinse my mouth with water, then brush my teeth, but after spitting out the toothpaste, the feeling returns, and I'm back at the toilet.

I've had the IUD for six months and haven't had a period since, so I can't be pregnant. I must have caught a cold. I shower, and afterward, I feel so much better that I'm even more baffled by the sickness.

I work on my computer for a couple of hours and make myself some lunch, wondering if something made me sick from dinner last night. Another thought comes to mind—Jude squeezing my breasts last night, and it hurt a little. I grab my breasts. My nipples are sensitive.

No.

I can't be.

There's no way.

My chest feels tight, and I have to work hard to draw in a breath. My heart races as I think through all the repercussions if I am pregnant, but then I tell myself to calm down. There's only one way to find out, and there's no sense freaking out until I know for sure.

An hour later, after buying a pregnancy test—not in downtown Willowbrook, but a neighboring town—and peeing on a stick, I know why I threw up this morning.

I'm pregnant.

And I have no idea how Jude will react to the fact that we're going to have a baby.

My hand falls to my stomach. A baby. Something I always wished for, but I thought I'd be married. I mean, I am, but it's not the same. We're just getting started together, finding our way as a couple. We haven't talked about what the next steps for us might be. And now I have to tell him he's going to be a father.

Chapter Twenty-Seven

JUDE

Sadie's on the couch at five thirty when I return to the house. I want a date night with her, but today was a shit day, and I'd really prefer to curl up on the couch with her in my arms, but she deserves for me to pull out all the stops, bad day or not.

She has a dress on, her computer on her lap as usual. She smiles at me, but something feels off about it. It's not the smile I'm used to getting lately.

"Hey, you look beautiful." I step over and kiss her lips. She kisses me back, but she doesn't put her hand on the back of head, keeping me in place for a few extra seconds, like she normally does. "I'm going to shower."

"Okay."

I walk up the stairs, a sour feeling in my stomach.

She was normal yesterday after Melody left. I'll never look at my tractor without getting a hard-on again. But could Melody's insistence that Sadie hasn't lived out her dream be on her mind? Has she realized that she's settling for a lesser life in Willowbrook with me? Maybe she's thinking more about what she wants in the future.

I hate the fear that invades the minute she's not my cheer-ful, happy girl. But I've always wanted Sadie to get out of this town. I always knew she was meant to be something bigger than a farmer's wife.

I take my shower and get ready, putting on fresh jeans and a button-down shirt. I made us reservations at the fancy Italian place in Hickory. I'm not usually a pasta guy, but Sadie loves it, and it's the fanciest place around here, which isn't saying much.

I walk down the stairs, and Sadie's still sitting in the same spot, her computer open, but she's looking out the window at the lake.

"Everything okay?" I ask.

She doesn't answer.

"Sadie." I sit on the couch and put on my boots.

She blinks and smiles at me.

"You okay?"

She nods. "I'm good. Are you ready?" She puts her computer on the coffee table, closes it, and stands to put on her sandals.

I drag her into me with my arm around her waist. "Are you sure? You seem upset."

Tell me, Sadie. I can take it.

"I'm perfect." She kisses me. "Come on, I don't want to be late."

She leaves the house first, and I grab my wallet and keys off the table by the door. Unlike normal, she walks down the stairs to my truck without waiting for me. At least she stands by the passenger door. I open it for her and help her up into my truck. I head to the driver's side, my mind a tornado whirling with all the reasons why Sadie could be so preoccupied right now.

When we pull into the parking lot, Sadie's shoulders sink. "This is too nice, Jude."

I squeeze her hand. "Nothing is too good for you."

This time, I do get one of her smiles, which eases some of the discomfort in my chest.

We walk hand in hand, and I open the door for her, placing my palm on the small of her back. At the hostess stand, she steps into me, getting closer, and I wrap my arm around her waist. Maybe I'm imagining things. She's had off days even before we were together, and I didn't give them this much headspace. She's not going to be in a good mood every day of our life. It could be her dad is on her mind, or she's worried about the chicken farm.

When the hostess leads us to our table, I pull out Sadie's chair for her, then fold myself into my own. She reads the menu, and a waitress comes over. I order us a bottle of wine although red isn't my favorite, but it feels right.

Once we've ordered, the waitress brings us the wine.

"Are you sure you're okay?" I ask, staring at Sadie's full glass of wine.

"I'm fine. I just haven't been feeling that great today."

"We could've stayed home."

"No." Her hand takes mine on the table, squeezing it. "I'm glad we came out."

"I drew up a blueprint for the chicken coop. Is there anything you wanted to modify on the first one I did?" Maybe talking about the chicken farm will boost her mood.

"I was thinking that maybe we could put a food tray along the one side," she says.

While we wait for our food, we talk about the chicken coops and what we need to add and remove. How we'll transport them around the land. And her mood does pick up a bit. She seems excited about making them this winter.

Our food arrives, and Sadie asks the waitress for an iced tea.

When I stare at her confused, she says, "I just don't want heartburn. Alcohol and red sauce." She shudders.

I nod, but don't say anything. I don't really want to talk about Melody and her bullshit, but I need to know what's going on in Sadie's head.

"Melody get home okay?" I ask.

She twirls her pasta around her fork. "Yeah, she texted me. Said she had to go right to the courthouse and change in the bathroom." She piles the forkful into her mouth.

"She sure is busy."

She nods and swallows. "Fast-paced life for sure."

"She has help though."

She looks at me as though she doesn't understand.

"The nanny."

"Well, she can't do it all, Jude." Her snippy remark takes me back for a second.

"I wasn't implying it was a bad thing."

"Sorry," she says instantly. "I'm just lost in my own thoughts tonight."

"About?"

She puts another forkful of pasta into her mouth. I sip the wine, waiting for an answer. No matter what it is, I want to know. I hate being in the dark.

"It's just everything. It's been a whirlwind these last couple of months, right? My dad dying, the wedding, me moving in."

My stomach clenches. "But you're happy?"

She rolls her eyes. "Why do people keep asking me that?"

"I don't mean to question it. I'm just curious."

She sits back in her chair. "I am. I wish people would believe me." She buries her head in her pasta.

I move my food around my plate, wishing we would've postponed this dinner.

"Can I ask you a question?"

I put down my fork, wipe my mouth with my napkin, and

give her my full attention. Finally, she's going to tell me what's really wrong.

"Where are we going?"

I tilt my head and study her. "What do you mean?"

She looks around for anyone paying us extra attention. Leaning over the table, she lowers her voice. "We're technically fake married."

Her statement is like a quick slice of a knife to the heart. Sure, we decided to get married before we started dating, but it doesn't make what we have any less real. We're just getting started. "I like being married to you."

She smiles and accepts my outstretched hand. "I like being married to you, but our future? What do you think it looks like?"

I feel as if it's a loaded question, as if she's looking for a specific answer, the way her eyes are lasered on me across the candlelit table.

"I like us now. We'll take it as it comes," I say.

I squeeze her hand. She gives me a wan smile and slides her hand away, picking up her fork. We finish our meal, not talking much, and head back home. The anxious tension in my body increases with every minute that ticks by.

We're no sooner in the house than she's heading to the stairs. I assume she's going to change out of her dress, but she turns to me at the bottom of the stairs.

"I'm going to head to bed. I'm tired."

"Are you feeling okay?" I ask, feeling as though I've been on repeat all night.

"Yeah." She breaks the distance, giving me a kiss. "Thanks for the date night. The pasta was great."

"You're welcome. I'll be up in a bit."

Her hand runs down my chest. "Take your time. Good night."

Turning around, I watch her walk up the stairs, my heart

aching because even though I just got her, I think I'm losing her.

§

I'VE GIVEN SADIE ALL WEEKEND TO TELL ME WHAT'S bothering her, and I've got nothing. She didn't want to start a new crime show on Saturday night. She was out of bed before me on Sunday, and I found her on the porch, sipping her tea and staring at the lake. She stayed at her mom's most of the day Sunday, helping her mom clear out some of her dad's things.

My only saving grace is that she cuddles up to me at night. But I laid awake most of last night, my mind reeling, thinking she's torn between staying with me here and taking some job in Los Angeles like Melody suggested. That stupid fear that I might be holding her back keeps popping up in my head like a flashing red warning sign.

I walk into the house at the end of the day Sunday, and she's in the kitchen making dinner.

"I could've cooked," I say, since I was always the one who did it before she moved in. Sometimes we cooked together, but I like preparing her meals. Especially her favorite.

She shrugs. "I'm home."

I wash my hands and wind them around her. She leans back into me, which is another good sign. She doesn't ever pull away from my affection.

"Let me finish." I rest my chin on top of her head.

"I've got it. I know you want to shower."

I kiss the top of her head. "I'll be right back."

In the shower, I have a hard time letting this go. What is she so upset about? I finish washing and open the shower door and startle when I find Sadie sitting on the counter.

"We have to talk."

Fucking finally. I was ready to go down there and demand she talk.

"What about?" I try to keep my voice casual.

"Just promise me, you won't shut down." Her hands are on either side of her thighs, her ankles crossed. She's in joggers and a sweatshirt.

"Okay," I say, bracing for the news, feeling bile rush up my throat. She's going to tell me she wants to explore her possibilities outside of Willowbrook.

"I need to know where this is going with us."

My eyebrows draw down. "That's the question?"

Her shoulders deflate, and she moves her hands into her lap, fiddling with them. I wrap the towel around my waist and walk over to her.

"Yes. I want to know what's going on. We're married but not really."

"We're married," I say.

"But—"

"I thought we were going through the motions, moving forward at our own pace. I'm not sure why we have to create a detailed plan." A forced laugh leaves my lips.

She doesn't return it.

Clearly, that was the wrong answer on my part.

"We can't just keep pretending." She slides off the counter as I'm about to touch her.

"Who's pretending?" I circle around, following her out of the bathroom.

"Our wedding wasn't real, Jude. Sure, we're together, but what do you want for our future?"

"Why don't you tell me the real question you're asking?" I grab my sweats and a T-shirt out of the drawer.

"Excuse me?" She sits on the bed, her legs crossed, her eyes barely meeting mine.

"What do *you* want?"

She throws her hands in the air. "You're going to throw the question back at me?"

"You're not acting yourself. Ever since Melody—"

"Melody has nothing to do with this. It's a simple question, Jude. What. Do. You. Want?"

I shake my head. "I want you to be happy."

"What else?"

"Am I supposed to want something else?"

She stands from the bed. "No, I guess not. Dinner's ready. I'm going on a walk around the lake."

She jogs down the steps, and the front door shuts behind her before I have one leg into my sweats.

I have no idea what she's looking for, but I'm fairly sure it's not me or Willowbrook.

Chapter Twenty-Eight

SADIE

I'm not in the mood to go to The Hidden Cave, but it's Lottie's birthday and probably one of the last nights we can be outside on the patio until the spring.

Jude is pissing me off. I know I'm acting weird, but I feel as if I can't control my emotions. I want to tell him, but I'm so scared. Jude's never said he doesn't want kids, but I feel as though I'm cornering him this early into whatever this is between us. I don't know how he'll react, and I'm afraid to tell him.

Plus, I wanted to wait to tell him until after I went to the doctor today to confirm the pregnancy and to ask how the hell I got pregnant when I had an IUD. Supposedly, they fall out of some people, and when she did my exam, she confirmed I'm one of those lucky folks. So while I thought we were having protected sex, we weren't. Awesome.

Jude parks in the lot of The Hidden Cave, and I wait for him to open my door. To anyone, we probably look like a happy couple, but emotions stew beneath our smiles and touches. I should just spit it out. Come what may. Surely it will be better than this constant tension between us.

We walk in and go to the back, his hand on my lower back the entire time. When we get to the patio, we find Lottie standing on one of the picnic tables, everyone around her singing "Happy Birthday."

"Sadie!" she shouts, clearly half-drunk already.

"Get the hell down before you hurt yourself," Brooks says.

Lottie rolls her eyes and shoos him away, stepping down from the table and heading our way. She wraps me in a tight hug. "Shot time." Then she moves over to Jude. "Hey, cuz." She hugs him and grabs my hand. "Come on."

I didn't even think about how I was going to get out of drinking tonight. Lottie doesn't drink alone and is usually the instigator of a good time at parties, which usually means shots and drinks.

"I'm not drinking. I have an early morning."

She drops my hand and stares at me. "You scheduled something for the day after my birthday?"

I cringe. "Sorry, but I'm here, aren't I?"

Jude leaves my side to huddle with his brothers and cousins. I'm glad to be away from the awkwardness between us lately, even if I'm the reason for it.

"Yes, you are." She hugs me again, and I smell the alcohol on her breath.

"Stop serving her, Melvin," Brooks says to the owner's son who sits at the end of the bar every night.

"She's fine," he says and winks at Lottie.

She blows him a kiss. "Dance with me."

Lottie takes her shot, and before I get my water, she drags me to the makeshift dance floor in front of the tables. While we dance, Romy and Laurel join in with Scarlett and Poppy. This family does love to party. We're in a circle, singing the words to the song, jumping up and down, bobbing our heads, and it feels good to get out of my head for a bit.

Then the song ends, and I look around, finding Jude staring at me. He's at the silo bar with Ben and his cousins, his elbows resting on the bar and his gaze on me. He doesn't smile and why should he? Things have been crap between us since I found out I was pregnant.

My hand slips down as if on instinct, but I stop it before I rub my stomach, a dead giveaway. I offer Jude a smile, and he tips the top of his beer at me, winking. But it's not his usual one. It's forced. I'm getting his forced smiles, and it breaks my heart.

"Are you okay?" Gillian shouts in my ear. She must've just joined us.

I nod. "Fine."

She studies me for a second and narrows her eyes, giving me an expression as if to say that if I need to talk, I know where to find her. "The Noughton boys are complicated."

Did she hear something? Is Jude at the bar complaining about me?

The next song is a slow song, so I leave the dance area.

Ben passes me. "Hey, Sadie."

I turn to see him grab Gillian by the waist, tugging her back onto the dance floor. They slow dance, and my heart pricks because Jude and I should be there.

"Come on." Jude comes up from behind me and slides his hand in mine, dragging me back to the dance floor.

"But you hate to dance."

"Not with you I don't." He pulls me into his arms, his hands wrapping around my waist.

I slide my hands up his neck and rest my head on his chest. He leads us around the dance floor, and I keep my eyes closed, loving the feeling of being in his arms. I want to be with him forever. Have as many babies as we're fortunate to have, grow old, and sit on the porch. I want the rest of my life to be with

Jude. And I'm pretty sure he wants that too. So why have I been so scared to tell him?

As the song slows, I stare at him. His eyes are already on me, and he tucks a strand of hair behind my ear.

"Jude," I say, and I can tell that he knows I'm finally going to tell him what's been going on with me. We can get through this. I know we can.

His finger comes to my lips. "It's okay. I understand."

My forehead wrinkles. Does he know?

Not allowing me to speak, he continues. "Go to Los Angeles. I'll take over the chicken farm."

Blinking a few times, it takes me a beat to answer. I step out of his arms. "What?"

"I know you want to go. Melody being here, hearing what her life is like...the job she said she could get you. It's okay. You deserve it. I'll hold things down here."

He reaches for me, but I wiggle away. "Do you want me to go?" My voice is a little loud, and Jude steps forward and lowers his head. "Jesus, Jude!"

The music stops, and Lottie comes over to my side. "Lovers' quarrel. They'll be fine. They're Jude and Sadie. Muusssiiiccc!" She puts up her hand and twirls her finger around.

Jude pins me with a stare. "I'm not sure why you're mad. I'm stepping aside. Giving you what you want."

I cannot believe him. "What makes you think I want Los Angeles?"

He shrugs. "I overheard Melody telling you how talented you are. You deserve to have that career you wanted in high school, the success. You deserve to have it all, Sadie."

I shake my head, tears gathering in my eyes. "Why am I so dispensable to you?"

"You're not," he says, stepping forward. "I love you."

"Yet you're so quick to push me out of your life with the

excuse of it being about *my* happiness. Maybe it's you, Jude. You're afraid. You're scared." I stab him in the chest with my finger.

"Scared of what? I don't understand. I'm telling you it's okay to go. Giving you permission."

I throw my arms in the air and stare at the dark sky.

"Hey, you two, maybe you want to go home and talk about this?" Gillian puts her hand on my back and eyes all the townspeople listening to us.

Anger boils my blood, and all the pent-up emotions from the past week flood out of me. "Tell them, Jude."

"Don't, Sadie." He shakes his head, lips thin.

"Hey, everyone, guess what?" I look around the crowd.

"Sadie," Jude bites out.

"Our marriage." I look at Jude. "It's not real. He married me so he could cosign the loan to save my family's farm."

"I knew it!" someone shouts.

"Yep, you win." A tear slips down my cheek as I look at Jude. "It was all fake."

His jaw tics. "Maybe it was just fake to you." He stomps away from me. "Ben, get her home."

Jude weaves through the crowd but stops at The Canary Post, the gossip board where people can write about anything going on in the gossip mill. He looks at a card, scowls at it, then tears it off.

"Hey, man!" Melvin calls.

"Fuck off," he says, tearing it in half and letting it fall to the ground.

Jude goes inside as Gillian says, "Hey, let's go."

"I'll take an Uber. You guys stay here." I walk through the now-quiet crowd, everyone's eyes on me as I stop and pick up the notecard.

You're all wrong. I saw Jude and Sadie at

the grocery store, and he stopped and kissed her in the frozen food section. They're in love. Everyone who thinks their marriage is a sham is dead wrong. Jude Noughton is off the market. Sorry, ladies.

Chapter Twenty-Nine

JUDE

I had to get out of The Hidden Cave last night after Sadie told everyone our wedding was fake. Couldn't stand to see all their judgmental looks. She never came home last night, and I assume she's at the cottage. So I knock on her door.

It opens, and I thank God she's not so mad that she's not going to open the door. Until I see Lottie standing in the doorway, looking as though she's sporting a pretty bad hangover. She slips through the opening.

"Lottie," I say with a nod.

She puts her hand on my chest, pushing me back. "You need to give her some space."

I scowl at my cousin. "No."

She looks back at the cottage, then at me. "She isn't ready to talk to you."

I stuff my hands in my pockets. "I don't understand. I only want what's best for her."

She tugs on my arm and pulls me off the stoop and away from the cottage. "Listen, from what I gather, she really wants you to figure yourself out. She loves you, but you have to trust her when she tells you something."

My forehead wrinkles. "What do you mean?"

Lottie sighs. "She's where she wants to be. You think she doesn't want to be here no matter how many times she tells you differently."

"Because—"

"Just give her some time. Think about what I said and maybe in a few days..." She cringes and rubs my arm. "I'll try to do some convincing, okay? But maybe just think about why you think you know better than her what makes her happy."

"Lottie," I plead, not wanting to go. My chest feels as if it's cracking open. Sadie's never iced me out like this.

She nods. "I know, but she's not going to see you today."

My throat burns as I say, "Tell her I love her, and I'm sorry."

"She knows."

I huff and wait a second as if Sadie's going to come to the door, but Lottie just gives me that pitiful smile of hers. So I walk back around her mom's house and climb into my truck, then drive away from the woman who is my entire life.

❦

"I PROBABLY FUCKED THIS UP," I SAY TO TITAN, running a brush over his mane.

"You did fuck it up," Dad says, coming into the stall and leaning his body against the wooden frame. "Get him ready to ride. Family meeting."

I groan. "You have to be kidding me."

"Yay, a family meeting." Ben raises his fist in the air in sarcasm, going to get Magnum.

Emmett's already got Brutus by the reins, all saddled up. When did they all get here?

"Fake marriage? What a disappointment." Emmett shakes his head, walking Brutus out of the barn.

I saddle Titan and lead him outside. Dad's already out there on Legend. Ben follows me.

"Again, you cockblock me," Ben grumbles.

"Stop it, you two."

Dad trots Legend to the path that leads to Mom's gravesite. It's a family plot that has a white picket fence surrounding it and a hill of daisies for my mom. No one says anything, and I'm thankful for the break from talking as we follow the beaten-down trail up the hill. After securing our horses, we each walk through the gate.

Dad approaches Mom's grave first. "You were right, Daisy. He loves her, but he's about to ruin it all." He kisses his fingers and presses them to the headstone.

I go next since we do everything in birth order.

"All I want is for her to be happy. Love you." I kiss my fingers and press them on top of her tombstone.

Ben follows me. "I tried to tell everyone, but no one listened. Don't worry about me. I figured all my shit out and couldn't be happier." He kisses his fingers and places them on the stone, smirking at me as he comes to stand beside me.

"Momma, I miss you. None of them have their shit together. I see why I was your favorite." Emmett bends down and kisses the stone top before hugging it.

Ben and I groan, rolling our eyes.

Emmett sinks down to the ground beside her, and the rest of us stand.

"Jude, you've always walled off your emotions. Too responsible for your own good." My dad starts the conversation as he always does for these family meetings. "I'm not sure, maybe you'd be different if your mom didn't die so young. But I shouldn't have to trick you into marrying the girl you love."

"What?" My mouth drops open.

"Oh, come on. You didn't know?" Emmett sneers.

"You think we're all that stupid?" Ben shakes his head.

Holy shit, they set me up.

"You've loved Sadie all these years. Hell, you've acted like you were her boyfriend the majority of your life. I thought you got that head out of your ass a few years ago, but you let her go off to New York and never told her. Even when she came back. So, sure you married her to secure the loan." Dad rolls his eyes.

"You mean you would've signed the loan without the marriage?" I ask, incredulous.

"Doesn't matter what I would've done. The fact is that you fought me on it, and you did marry her. That's not very Jude-like to anyone other than Sadie. Seeing you two the last couple months or so, we're all aware that something changed."

I take off my cowboy hat and run my hand through my hair. "Yeah. We finally—"

"No details!" Emmett raises his hand.

"Grow up," Ben says.

"I'm not asking to compare dick sizes," I say.

"Enough," Dad snaps. "I'm glad for whatever got you... well, I assume it's Sadie that got you to admit your feelings. But then whatever has happened to get you lost in that damn head of yours, forget it. You're about to ruin it all."

Ben clamps my shoulder. "You know you deserve happiness, right?"

My brothers and I are rarely serious with one another. Up here at the family meetings might be the only time.

I shrug him off. "She should be far away from here."

"But she's not," Ben says.

"Have you ever asked her?" my dad asks. "A conversation can clear up a lot of shit that clogs your brain. It's like a laxative for your thoughts." When I don't say anything, he sighs and sets his hands on his hips. "Son, why do you think you're not good enough for her?"

"Because he's Jude," Emmett says.

I shake my head. "I don't know. I just want her to have

everything she's ever wanted. She...had to stay back after college. When she finally got out, she had to come back because her grandma died."

"Are you sure about that?" Dad asks and quirks his eyebrow.

"Do you know something?"

"It's not my story to tell."

I rack my brain for the memory of when I asked her about coming back, but nothing stands out.

"For some reason that even Einstein couldn't figure out, she wants you, Jude, and you just keep pushing her away. One day you're going to push her away completely." Ben stares at me.

I read Mom's tombstone. She was way too young when she died. "We only have so many years on this earth. Some lives are shorter than others. I don't want her to have regrets. Wake up one day and look at me and think about the would've, could've, should'ves."

Dad laughs, shaking his head at me like I'm an idiot.

Ben joins in.

Emmett picks at the grass.

"I'm not like Ben. I don't show my emotions. I'm a pissy, moody son of a bitch."

"Not with Sadie," Emmett says and nods when I look at him. "Not with her, you're not."

"Yeah, you could slit our throats with a look, but Sadie doesn't get that side of you. She gets this Jude that no one recognizes," Ben says.

"You can't always figure out why someone loves you, son. Sometimes I'm not sure how I got your mother to fall in love with me. That was a miracle in and of itself. And there's so much I regret every day. Fights we had. Times when I didn't rush home to her. But everyone here knows that Sadie loves you, Jude. And you love her. I probably should've hugged you more, told you how great you were, but I was trying to raise you..." Dad stops talking and swallows hard. "Somewhere, I missed it."

I look at him. "What?"

Ben gives me a look like I should already know what Dad's talking about.

Dad clears his throat. "I missed teaching you that you deserve to be loved. That you're enough. I think maybe that's something a mom gives her child. Unconditional love. Whereas I always made demands of you and wanted you to be responsible."

"Don't blame yourself. Jude's the only messed up one of the three of us." Emmett gives me a wide smile.

Fucker.

"Let her love you, Jude. Let yourself be her number one." I fight back tears as my dad continues. "You're enough, son. You're a great man, hardworking, honest, and caring."

I want so badly to push past my barriers. So badly.

"You're gonna make me cry." Emmett pretends to wipe a tear.

"Go get your girl," Ben says. "I know you're not used to groveling but get those knees dirty."

I stand there for a minute, letting everything they said settle in my brain until I know they're right. And I know what I have to do.

"You straight now?" my dad asks.

I nod. "Yeah. Thanks."

"One of us was bound to be screwed up. Sorry it was you." Emmett stands, knowing it's time for a group hug.

"Fuck off."

"Huddle time," dad says.

We circle Mom's tombstone, linking our arms and staring at it.

"Love you," we say in unison.

Back on our horses, we're quiet on the ride back down the hill.

I'm not sure I'd ever have my head on straight if it wasn't for my brothers and dad. I'm pretty sure I'll always fear Sadie wanting more than I can offer her, but she knows what she wants. If she's happy with me, who the hell am I to argue?

Chapter Thirty

SADIE

Lottie knocks on my door. "Yoo-hoo! You ready? Let's go." She comes into the small hallway of my cottage and stands outside my bathroom. "Dropped another delivery off." She cringes and eyes the kitchen table where the other deliveries she's dropped off over the past couple of days sit.

I finish curling my hair, ducking my head out of the bathroom to see another bouquet of wildflowers and a note from Jude.

He's left one on my porch each morning.

The first note said he was sorry and wanted to talk when I was ready.

The second note said he loved me and realized what a fool he was for not seeing what he sees now. Asking again to talk so he can grovel like he should.

I step out of the bathroom and walk over to the wildflower bouquet. Little does he know the smell of them makes me nauseated.

I open the letter and read his scrawling handwriting.

Sadie,

Our house is too empty. Our bed is too cold. I miss you.

Yours always,
Jude

Lottie snags the card and drops it on the table. "Time to go." She grabs her purse and walks to the door.

"Calling me this morning and saying you're taking me to lunch isn't a lot of notice." I come to a stop when I see my mom standing by Lottie's car. "What's going on?"

"Oh, I invited your mom. She needs to get out of the house."

My mom shrugs. "I can always do lunch."

I nod and shut the door of the cottage.

I let Mom have the front seat, and I sit in the back, Jude's last letter rolling over and over in my mind. I pull out my phone.

I'll be by this evening.

The three dots appear immediately, and my heart warms as though maybe he was waiting for me to text him.

I won't be home. How about tomorrow?

Tomorrow? Seriously? For a guy who has been begging to see me, he's willing to wait until tomorrow?

I stuff my phone back in my purse before I text something angry.

Lottie steers the car onto the highway.

"Where are we going?" I ask.

"I told you. Lunch." She eyes me in the rearview mirror.

"Where?"

"Lincoln." She smiles at me.

"Oh, I love Lincoln," Mom says. "I needed a day out. Thanks for the invite, Lottie." She pats Lottie's leg and straightens in her chair as if she can't contain her excitement.

At least one of us is excited.

I sulk in the back seat, pissed that Jude is too busy to talk to me tonight and that Lottie hijacked me to take me to Lincoln. Maybe Hickory I would have been okay with, but Lincoln?

God, these pregnancy hormones are making me cranky.

She pulls into their downtown area forty-five minutes later and parks at a meter. Mom and I climb out and stand on the sidewalk, waiting for Lottie to direct us where to go. She goes to her trunk.

"I'm starving, let's go," I whine.

She shuts her trunk, holding another bouquet of flowers and a note.

I blink at the flowers. "What's this?"

She looks up at the sign of the store in front of us, then back at me. I follow her line of sight and gawk. It's a bridal salon. Mannequins in gorgeous white dresses are displayed in the window.

"I don't understand," I say.

Lottie hands me the flowers and the note. "We'll be waiting inside if you decide to come in." She swings her arm around my mom's and escorts her into the store.

I place the flowers on the roof of Lottie's car, and my hands shake as I pull out the note. This note is the longest of them all.

Sadie,

I'm so out of my comfort zone right now, but

if it means I can win you back, I'll do it a hundred times over.

I've been an idiot. But you already figured that out. I love you, and I thought I knew better than you what you needed. Truth is, I don't feel worthy of your love, but I'm trying to work on that. You're made for greatness, and I felt like staying in Willowbrook and being a farmer's wife wasn't enough. That's MY problem, not yours. I realize now that the love we share is something rarely found, and it needs to be cherished and nurtured—not managed and strong-armed.

I've been the happiest I've ever been in my life since I married you. Admitting my feelings and sharing my life with you has made me love life in a way I didn't before. You're on my mind when I plow the fields, when I herd the cattle, and when I'm cursing Emmett for doing something stupid. I can't wait to get home every night, and I dread leaving you in bed every morning. My life is nothing without you.

If you can find it in your heart to forgive me, please go into that bridal salon and try on a million dresses. They assure me you can have one off the rack and they'll do whatever adjustments are needed to have you wear it tonight.

Pick the one you love and meet me at The Knotted Barn at five thirty. I'll be standing at the end of the aisle waiting to be your husband...again. For real this time.

I'll be waiting.

Love always,
Jude

With tears in my eyes and love in my heart, I fold up the note and slide it into my purse. I smile when I remember his text saying that he was busy tonight. I shake my head with a smile. And he thinks he's not funny.

I open the door to the bridal salon, and everyone cheers when I go inside.

Gillian, Romy, Scarlett, Poppy, Laurel, Lottie, and my mom are all waiting for me, each holding up a dress.

"Ready to try on some dresses?" my mom asks. I walk over to her, nodding, and her hand cradles my cheek when I reach her. "He's a lucky man."

Tears fall from my eyes. "We're both lucky."

"Yeah, you are."

❧

At exactly five thirty that evening, I link my arm through my mom's and walk down the aisle to once again marry Jude. This ceremony is only for our closest friends and family, which I'm happy about. The wedding wasn't important, and I realize that now. Marrying Jude and being able to spend the rest of my life with him is what matters.

After we say our vows and we're announced as husband and wife, we walk down the aisle.

In the bridal suite, Jude takes me in his arms and kisses me again. "I'm so sorry, Sadie."

"You're all I want," I say. "I just wanted you to see that."

"And I do. I know you love me, but I didn't want you ever to have regrets."

I put my hands on his cheeks and make him look at me. "As long as I have you, there are no regrets. I've wasted all these years hiding my feelings. Jude, I went to New York, and I *hated* it. I missed you and my life in Willowbrook. I was too ashamed to tell anyone, but I don't want that life. And I told Melody that before she left."

"I figured she had everything you'd ever wanted, and I got scared."

"Are you married to Melody?" I shake my head. "No."

"Why do you put up with me?" He drops his forehead to mine.

"That's easy. I love you, and I know how much you love me. I know you want me to experience everything this world offers, but I don't want to do that without you. Willowbrook is where our love sprouted, and I want here to be where it grows. Trust me, okay?"

He nods, brushing a kiss against my forehead. "I trust you."

"Good. Now let's go celebrate our wedding...again." I laugh.

He captures my lips, and our kiss gets a little heavy before we part. "I can't wait to have makeup sex tonight."

"I doubt it will beat our first wedding night." I move to walk out of the room.

"You doubting me, Mrs. Noughton?"

"Never." I smile and hold my hand out for him.

We join our family, and when it's time for our first dance, "Your Everything" by Keith Urban plays.

Jude leads me around the dance floor in his arms. "I'm sorry, Sadie."

"Stop apologizing. All of this more than makes up for it. Thank you for arranging the dress shopping."

He chuckles. "But you wore your original dress."

I shrug. "It's sentimental."

He circles us around. "I wanted you..." He seems to stop himself from whatever he was going to say. Probably something about how I always wanted to go dress shopping. "I love the dress. It's beautiful."

I grin at him. "Good answer, Mr. Noughton."

"I'm learning, Mrs. Noughton."

"There's something I need to tell you." I had planned to wait until we got home tonight, but the longer we're face to face, the harder it becomes to hold it in.

He stops dancing for a second and inspects my face before moving us again. "You're scaring me."

"I'm...pregnant."

This time, he stops dancing completely. He stares at me, his eyes crinkling. "Really? How?" He shakes his head, disbelieving.

"I know it's a surprise, and it's a long story, but—"

"Sadie..." His voice is a soft rasp.

Jude falls to his knees on the dance floor, both hands going to my hips, and presses his lips to my stomach. My hands wind through his hair as he looks up at me with tears in his eyes. A few gasps echo through the room, then the cheering and clapping start.

"Baby Noughton! Man, he just beat you on all fronts!" Emmett shouts to Ben.

Our guests all laugh.

Jude stands back up on his feet. "Thank you."

"For what?"

"For giving me everything I've ever wanted but was too stubborn to fight for until now."

His lips come down on mine, and we seal our forever with a kiss.

Epilogue

JUDE

Sadie and I walk into my dad's house on Sunday morning, and there's a brunette wearing my dad's flannel shirt at the table. I wince and groan.

"Hi, I'm Sadie," my wife says. "And this is Jude."

The brunette seems alarmed by our intrusion but shakes Sadie's hand. "I'm Janice."

"Hi, Dad." Sadie walks over to the stove where he's scrambling eggs for his lady friend and kisses his cheek, then steals a cheese danish.

"Why are you here this early?" Dad asks.

"I have to borrow your UTV because mine is at the shop," I say.

"Where are you two going?" he asks.

"Um..." I eye Janice and offer her a small smile.

"To see Daisy," Sadie says, giving a vague enough answer that the woman here might not realize we're going to see my mom. She rubs her swollen belly with a smile.

"Glad you told me. I would've spoiled the news. Managed to keep it to myself this long, but that was gonna come to an end." He continues to work at the stove.

Emmett walks in, apparently unfazed by the woman's presence as he says over his shoulder, "You owe me. We made a bet."

Ben's right behind him.

"Why are you two here? This is why I made you move out and build your own houses," Dad grumbles.

"What was the bet?" I ask, sitting on a chair and patting my leg for Sadie.

She sits down and offers me a bite of her danish.

"That you'd be engaged by the end of this season." Emmett smiles proudly. "He's been dodging me for months."

"And they got married at the end of *last* season. So, you lost." Ben sits down next to me.

"Will you two stop arguing?" Gillian says, walking in with Clayton right behind her.

"Why am I here?" Clayton asks in the way that only a put-upon teenager can.

Janice's eyes widen as she looks around at all the new faces.

Gillian sits on Ben's lap, and he kisses her.

Clayton groans. "Need any help, Bruce?"

Bruce puts Clayton to work.

"Ben's being a cheap-ass, Gillian," Emmett whines.

"I'd pay if you were right." He gives Emmett a smug smile.

Emmett grabs my left hand and holds it up. "I couldn't be any righter."

"You never said married. You said *engaged*. And you never said last season, you said *this* season. Wrong." Ben makes a buzzer sound.

"All right, boys, we have company." My dad stops the arguing as he usually does after he lets it go on for a while.

"Fine. Let's talk about Briar coming back to Willow-brook," Emmett says.

"Don't even think about it," Ben practically growls.

Gillian gives Emmett a nasty look.

"She's family." Emmett walks over and grabs himself a danish.

"Exactly," Gillian says.

I pat Sadie's ass to get up and stand after her.

"We're out," I say, not in the mood to sit around with Dad's Saturday night fling and the rest of my family. I love them, but Sadie and I have a plan to execute.

"Where are you going?" Emmett asks, taking the seat I vacated.

"None of your business," I say.

"Sadie?" He sounds like he used to when we didn't include him in something when we were younger. "Remember, I was your groom first."

I grab my dad's UTV keys, then Sadie's hand. "And I'm her last."

"He's got you there," Ben says.

Sadie and I leave, hearing them start a whole new argument as we go. It's how we Noughtons show love.

❧

I PARK THE UTV AT THE BOTTOM OF THE HILL. I'm not about to take any chances with Sadie riding a horse. It's cooler today and both of us are bundled in coats, hats, and gloves. Winter hasn't quite left us yet so I brought us a thick blanket to put on the ground so Sadie can relax while we're here.

We walk up the hill that's now empty of daisies to the fence surrounding the gravesites. I open the swinging gate and usher Sadie in before following and letting the gate shut. I lay the blanket on the ground and hold Sadie's hand to help her sit. She's always quick to remind me that she's fully capable of doing everything she could before she was pregnant, but I don't think that means I can't pamper her a little.

I sit beside her, and Sadie slides closer, putting her arm around my shoulders. My mind goes back to when we sat here twenty-eight years ago.

"We're opening a chicken farm this season," Sadie says, breaking the ice because she knows it's hard for me to start. "That might sound crazy, but I can't wait to wear one of those aprons to hold the eggs."

"Sadie's got the designs, and we built the chicken coops this winter so everything will be ready when the weather turns. We're both excited."

"Briar, Gillian's sister, is coming back. She's going to do some yoga classes for people who stay at The Getaway Lodge," Sadie says. "You might have to keep your eye out on your youngest, though."

I look at her, confused. What is she talking about?

"Jude's so blind sometimes, right?" Sadie laughs, looking at the gravestone. "Emmett struck out every at-bat last year when Briar was there, and he got all quiet and awkward after the game. He can't stop staring at her every time she comes into the room."

"I'm not sure they even like each other," I say. Sadie's wrong on this one.

"That doesn't mean they don't want one another. Or he wants her at least."

I do remember the ball hitting Emmett on the forehead when he first saw Briar, but that doesn't mean anything.

"You're wrong," I say. She has to be. Gillian would never let that happen.

"Want to bet?"

"Depends on the wager."

"One sexual act of my choosing." She puts out her hand.

I shake it. "Done."

"They'll be sleeping together before the end of the summer," she says.

"Damn, you're that sure?"

She nods and turns back to the gravestone, looking at me from the corner of her eye. "We have something else to tell you."

"Mom." I place my hand on Sadie's stomach. "We're having a baby."

The warmth from the sun feels hotter for a moment, and I like to think it's my mom telling me she hears me.

"And?" Sadie prods.

"It's a girl. We're going to name her Daisy." I attempt to push back the tears pooling in my eyes.

"I told you from the beginning that it was a girl."

Sadie insists her mother's intuition was giving her strong girl vibes early on in the pregnancy and turns out she was right.

"As long as you and the baby are healthy, that's all that matters." I kiss her temple, then look at my mom's headstone. "I'm so happy, Mom. The only thing that could make me happier would be if you were still here." A tear slips free, and I wipe it with my hand.

Sadie lays her head on my shoulder and kisses my jawline. "It's okay. I won't tell anyone."

The End

Next in the series is the lovable younger brother, Emmett Noughton. If you love an enemies-to-lovers, burned by love heroine, he falls first hero then this book is your jam!

Learn more about The One I Didn't See Coming at www.piperrayne.com

Also by Piper Rayne

A Greene Family Summer Bash (Novella)

My Sister's Flirty Friend

My Unexpected Surprise

My Famous Frenemy

A Greene Family Vacation (Novella)

My Scorned Best Friend

My Fake Fiancé

My Brother's Forbidden Friend

A Greene Family Christmas (Novella)

Lake Starlight

The Problem with Second Chances

The Issue with Bad Boy Roommates

The Trouble with Runaway Brides

The Drawback of Single Dads

Modern Love

Charmed by the Bartender

Hooked by the Boxer

Mad about the Banker

Single Dads Club

Real Deal

Dirty Talker

Sexy Beast

Hollywood Hearts

Mister Mom

Animal Attraction

Domestic Bliss

Bedroom Games

Cold as Ice

On Thin Ice

Break the Ice

Chicago Law

Smitten with the Best Man

Tempted by my Ex-Husband

Seduced by my Ex's Divorce Attorney

Blue Collar Brothers

Flirting with Fire

Crushing on the Cop

Engaged to the EMT

White Collar Brothers

Sexy Filthy Boss

Dirty Flirty Enemy

Wild Steamy Hook-up

The Rooftop Crew

My Bestie's Ex

A Royal Mistake

The Rival Roomies

Our Star-Crossed Kiss

The Do-Over

A Co-Workers Crush

Hockey Hotties

Countdown to a Kiss (Free Prequel)

My Lucky #13 (FREE)

The Trouble with #9

Faking it with #41

Tropical Hat Trick (Novella)

Sneaking around with #34

Second Shot with #76

Offside with #55

Kingsmen Football Stars

False Start (Free Prequel)

You Had Your Chance, Lee Burrows

You Can't Kiss the Nanny, Brady Banks

Over My Brother's Dead Body, Chase Andrews

Chicago Grizzlies

On the Defense (Free Prequel)

Something like Hate

Something like Lust

Something like Love

Holiday Romances

Single and Ready to Jingle

Claus and Effect

Cockamamie Unicorn Ramblings

Those of you who read our ramblings in every book know what we're going to say... another friends-to-lovers book! But this one was a little more fun because of their history and the fact that they've had a bond since they were six.

It's always hard to find ways for friends-to-lovers to cross over into more and we didn't want it to be about jealously caused by another man or woman in this case. We wanted it just to be life that just never allowed them to explore their feelings. We've all had that one person in our lives that we can't imagine not having around. That was Jude to Sadie, so we double-downed on that belief in keeping them as friends.

There isn't a lot that changed through the course of writing this book. The chicken farm was originally going to be a flower farm, but we have The Perfect Petal already as part of the ranch which will be part of another cousin's story.

Lottie wasn't going to be Sadie's best friend, but we loved the idea of getting more of her (and Brooks) on the page. You got to know Brooks in Ben's book and now Lottie in Jude's. This of course is so we can shamelessly tease you for their book! *both of us bat our eyelashes*

Emmett's book is next, and we promise you, you're going to get glimpses into some more of the cousins and even one of the aunts!

As always, we have a lot of people to thank for getting this book into your hands...

Nina and the entire Valentine PR team.

Cassie from Joy Editing for line edits who is probably really surprised we got her the book on time! LOL

Ellie from My Brother's Editor for line edits and proofing.

Hang Le for the cover and branding for the entire series which is SOOO beautiful.

Regina Wamba for the beautiful photo, giving us the inspiration for Jude and Sadie.

All the bloggers who graciously carve out time to read, review and/or promote us.

All the Piper Rayne Unicorns who give us a fun space online to chat and show us love on the daily!

Readers – With so many books out there, we're so thankful you've chosen ours. We hope you're excited to continue on in the series!

Emmett's life is about to get turned upside down with the arrival of Gillian's little sister, Briar. Of course, Gillian and Ben want him to stay far, far away from her. But as we all know from the first two books, Bruce Noughton wants his boys to find their happily ever after, and he makes it very difficult for Emmett not to notice that Briar might just be his perfect match.

xo,
 Piper & Rayne

About Piper & Rayne

Piper Rayne is a *USA Today* Bestselling Author duo who write "heartwarming humor with a side of sizzle" about families, whether that be blood or found. They both have e-readers full of one-clickable books, they're married to husbands who drive them to drink, and they're both chauffeurs to their kids. Most of all, they love hot heroes and quirky heroines who make them laugh, and they hope you do, too!

Printed in Great Britain
by Amazon